D1387855

LEAVES ON THE LINE

Martin & Simon Toseland

First published in the United Kingdom in 2013 by
Portico Books
10 Southcombe Street
London
W14 0RA

An imprint of Anova Books Company Ltd

ISBN 9781907554858

A CIP catalogue record for this book is available
from the British Library.

10 9 8 7 6 5 4 3 2 1

Printed and bound by 1010 Printing International Ltd, China

This book can be ordered direct from the publisher at
www.anovabooks.com

LEAVES ON THE LINE

Martin & Simon Toseland

What the British say ...
And what we really mean

PORTICO

AS BRITISH AS...
8

POLITICS
22

TRAVEL,
WEATHER &
ABROAD
46

WORK &
TRADE
32

CONTENTS

SPORT
62

BIRTHS,
MARRIAGES,
DEATHS &
RELATIONSHIPS
98

PETS
74

FOOD
112

FAMILY LIFE
82

SHOPPING
&
COMPLAINING
124

SORRY
138

HELLO!
NICE TO MEET YOU[1]

The British have long been renowned for their inability to master other languages. Perhaps that is because they have to learn at least two when they take on their native tongue. In every walk of life, from relationships, to work, to politics, sport and the news, our everyday English harbours duplicities of meaning. Our everyday behaviour surfs a troubled sea of motives and intentions.

'Sorry', 'Nice to meet you', 'Do you know what I mean?' These words and phrases are uttered millions of times every day. But how can you really know what the person means? When an MP says 'with respect' does he actually mean that he is respectful of a person's knowledge and expertise or does he mean, 'I'm an MP and you may have 20 years of experience but you don't have a minor job in government and a dodgy expenses claim so I'm going to completely ignore everything you have to say.' We say 'I'm sorry' when we mean 'absolute nonsense', and write 'Yours faithfully' when we're thinking 'Fuck you!' Jealousy, rage, love, affection – we're equally good at disguising them all.

The British load humdrum expressions with layers of meaning and nuance that can flummox even the most experienced linguist. It's not that all of these words, sentiments and situations are unique to Britain and the British, just that they are how we define ourselves to each other. The context and tone of voice provide cultural clues that no dictionary can help with.

So an American may, and almost certainly does, say 'Sorry' when they don't mean it, but not when they mean to say, 'I'm just looking for my credit card and in the meantime I'm embarrassed that I'm holding you up dreadfully by at least, oh, two or three seconds.' They won't say that either – or even think it. But that's another story. We'll say 'Sorry' because it's shorthand for these thoughts and fills in marvellously for having to make the effort to communicate clearly. This is why it's such a useful word.

Leaves on the Line, in hilarious and forthright terms, exposes the doublespeak of the British psyche. For the first time, characteristics and situations, and everyday terms that we casually deploy to loved ones and total strangers, have thrown at us from the radio and TV, or suffer from the mouths of politicians and estate agents, will be 'glossed' (yes, we really mean 'stripped') to reveal the unadorned, solid British oak that lies beneath. With no apologies for any offence caused. Sorry about that.

Simon and Martin Toseland, March 2013

---

1. This is the first of many lies we'll be looking at. It may very well be not nice to meet you. It may be one of the worst experiences of our entire lives. We have no way of telling yet. We'll get back to you.

To get us in the mood, let's have a look at some well-loved phrases, rituals and icons of our island life which collectively define the British to the world, and which might mortify us had they not become so integral to our existence over time that we've ceased to view them as in any way strange or disturbing. These are the colours on the artist's palette that help paint a picture of Britishness, or at least the shades of grey that make us what we are...

❝ A NICE CUP OF TEA ❞

A NICE CUP OF TEA is still, alongside 14 pints of farty lager, the average Briton's drug of choice – we drink well over 100 million cups a day for fuck's sake – it is the drink of Britain *nonpareil* (oops, that's French). Seen by many as a panacea for every situation – from the receipt of a parking fine to being the victim of an assault with a deadly weapon – tea is the calming, communal high cherished by everyone from the Hampshire vicar's wife to crack dealers in Toxteth: A NICE CUP OF TEA will always put the world to rights for a couple of minutes.

What Brits mean by A NICE CUP OF TEA is quite variable though: it can be half-milk, half-sugar; strongly brewed with the bag squeezed to within an inch of its life; or even black with a sour, tanniny aftertaste coating the mouth like tarmac. How you take it speaks volumes in our class-ridden country – the lighter and sweeter, the more, ahem, 'manual' your profession is assumed to be. And then of course there are the types of leaf – from the stalwart's English Breakfast to perfumed Earl Grey and then the more esoteric green and white and (uuurgh) fruit teas, which have been creeping into favour, it's safe to say there are more than 50 shades of tea for the adventurous, or masochistic, among us.

GETTING DRUNK

If we love one thing more than A NICE CUP OF TEA or GOING FOR A CURRY (see p.116), it may very well be getting badgered, bevvied, bluttered, clobbered, decimated, fecked, guttered, hammered, inebriated, juice-looped, lashed, mangled, out of it, paralytic, pickled, rat-assed, razzled, skinned, slaughtered, stocious, tabled, trashed, troll-eyed, tired and emotional, wasted, wellied, wankered, zombied or, to put it simply, DRUNK. If the Eskimo notoriously has 50 words for snow to choose from (not strictly true by the way, but never let a fact get in the way of a true story), then he may well be staggered, or even blitzed, to learn that we Brits have well over 800 words to describe the various incarnations of intoxication.

❝ KEEP A STIFF UPPER LIP ❞

One thing we're notorious for is our STIFF UPPER LIP – a hangover from Victorian times when the imperative in all actions was to demonstrate, as the *New Oxford American Dictionary* defines it, a quality of 'uncomplaining stoicism'. Regardless of the loss of limbs, relatives or dignity, the Victorian gentleman was expected to display at all times a *sang-froid* so chilly that his face could trigger another ice age. This demeanour became so prevalent that it stuck as perhaps our most famous characteristic – as if any sign of the lip quivering might bring the whole Empire down. Fast-forward 150 years or so and the lip configuration has shifted from stiff upper to blubbing lower. Our television screens are regularly filled with the unwholesome spectacle of incontinent British emotions. Game shows and talent competitions all require contestants to go on an emotional, tear-stained journey in front of the viewing public; while the passing of anyone (or anything – a pet is by no means exempt) who has endeared themselves to the smallest fraction of the population is treated as a national tragedy – invariably demonstrated by building a mountain of garage-bought flowers. The rigid gentlemen explorers of the Age of Empire would be spinning in their graves if their stiff upper lips allowed it.

❝ THE PUBLIC HAVE A RIGHT TO KNOW... ❞

'We're desperate to sell papers by any means – legal or otherwise – and if that means going through a few bins or bullying vulnerable people, you can rely on us.

'What do you mean, the nocturnal shenanigans of a Premier League footballer aren't in the public interest? Do you know how much these people get paid? Yes, he's a single man in his 20s engaging in a casual, sexual relationship with two young consenting women but we think that's saucy, and THE PUBLIC HAVE A RIGHT TO KNOW.

'How's that? A best-selling author doesn't want her new address published and 20 photographers taking pictures of her daughter leaving for school? Well, she should have thought about that before she became rich and famous, shouldn't she? Didn't mind the publicity when she was on the way up, did she? She thinks her privacy is being invaded? The public are interested in where she lives and how big her house is, so it's in the public interest, innit? THE PUBLIC HAVE A RIGHT TO KNOW.'

❝ I'M NOT BEING RACIST BUT... ❞

'...what I'm about to say will be so offensive to anyone of mixed or other race than white, or indeed anyone who doesn't secretly think that slavery might still be the answer to all our problems, that I might as well black up now, put on a cod Jamaican accent and have done with it.

'I'm only having a laugh, I'M NOT BEING RACIST BUT, you know, seriously, they come over here with their families and cousins, force us into marriage, take all our jobs and stink of curry. Don't get me wrong, I love a good curry, we invented it, didn't we? And now we have to give them aid and they've got a space programme. I'M NOT BEING RACIST BUT it's ridiculous, isn't it?'

❝ LOL ❞

The texting acronym 'LOL' isn't a peculiarly British expression – it's almost certainly American in origin and has two meanings, though, these days, 'Laugh Out Loud' has pretty much wiped out 'Lots Of Love', certainly among the under-50s. This can lead to some unintentionally upsetting texts from the older Brit, such as 'Sorry 2 hear your cat died. LOL.' The fact that our Prime Minister couldn't decide which one he meant when texting a disgraced former tabloid editor, also speaks volumes about being British.

❝ BOBBIES ON THE BEAT ❞

'They get younger every year don't they? We definitely need more BOBBIES ON THE BEAT – you see they get to know what's going on, they stay in touch with criminals, keep tabs on them, get backhanders – keep things under control.

'Nowadays, they're all volunteers aren't they? Riding around on their mountain bikes, turning up long after the crime's been committed and then spending three hours compiling a report that might as well read – "Burglary. Stuff taken. Case won't be solved. Burglar won't be arrested." All the real Bobbies have been let go, or retired. That's why crime's gone through the roof, people openly dealing drugs on the streets and stealing mobile phones. If we had more BOBBIES ON THE BEAT, they'd be grabbing these young drug dealers by their hoodies and giving them a cuff round the head and an earful of good, honest advice. And that would be an end to it.'

❝ SENSE OF FAIR PLAY ❞

The British SENSE OF FAIR PLAY is recognised throughout the world… as being yet another British delusion. When you have built an Empire on the proceeds gained from subjugating foreign peoples and stealing their resources, in exchange for a *Railway Timetables for Dummies* book, it's a bit rich to go all jolly hockey-sticks and rooting for the underdog when you see an unmatched contest. Still, we believe in it, so it must exist, right?

DANCING

The British have a complicated relationship with dancing. The Spanish have the flamenco, the Argentinians the tango, the Austrians have the waltz, while our traditional dance is the Morris – a ritual of leaden movement so painfully laden with fertility symbolism that it's no surprise we get embarrassed about it while sober, and keep it confined to remote villages where *The Wicker Man* looks like the vision of a bright and beautiful future world. The Morris Dance has its modern-day equivalent around half-past three in the morning in most city centres, as pissed-up youths on Meow Meow (or whatever they call it) stagger around clumsily looking for someone or something to shag. Yep, DANCING, we call it.

❛ LET ME MAKE IT CLEAR... ❜

We Brits have perfected the art of, to paraphrase Ronan Keating, 'saying it best when we say nothing at all'. We're also accomplished at the art of saying one thing but meaning something else – if irony and sarcasm were Olympic sports we'd get gold, silver and bronze every time. Americans are, by equal measure, fascinated and appalled by our ability to bumble through a conversation without making ourselves clear, or delivering a barbed remark that sails over the recipient's head and falls flat. It's why the world sees us as pompous while we see ourselves as urbane, sophisticated and, well, superior. God, we can be unbearable!

OUR LOVE OF COUNTRYSIDE

We love our countryside, the quilted pattern of yellow rape fields and minor-road networks that spread out from the out-of-town retail parks and intersect our tarmacked cities. We love nothing more than going for a long stroll in our countryside, dodging homicidal cows and the razor-sharp barbed wire that farmers lay on as a rural assault course for our pleasure.

We can't get enough of those remote country pubs that time forgot, with their quaint credit card readers and alcoholic bar-room bigots who would spray their foamy, warm beer all over the Thomas Hardy-style tiled floor if so much as a person of mixed race should cross the doorstep.

Indeed, OUR LOVE OF COUNTRY-SIDE is so great that we continue to smother it with high-speed rail-links, green-belt executive housing developments and seething rage-filled ring roads which effortlessly link one hypermarket with another and put the living fear of God into any foreign national reckless enough to stray from one place of outstanding natural beauty to the other.

Yes, OUR LOVE OF COUNTRYSIDE is double-edged, for we distrust it as much as we

revere it. For those considered 'townies', by the 15 or so remaining dairy farmers not already working their heifers to the bone for a multiple retailer, the countryside is a place where Bad Things Happen, like dropping to two-bar reception on your smartphone, or being unable to get an overpriced carton of coffee water within three minutes drive in any direction. For the townie this can quickly lead to a state of blind panic – what's the point of being out here if you can't update your Facebook status to let your townie friends know how intrepid and life-embracing you are ('Me in a field LOL')? Tweeting isn't just for the birds that used to fill the trees (sinister how the few remaining ones group together and stare at you).

Some isolated areas remain beacons of pure, unadulterated pastoral bliss, with no criss-crossing budget airline skytrails, no thundering of articulated lorries full of Ginster's pasties and no papier-mâché housing estates besmirching the rural idyll. The easiest way to find them is to search a map of Britain for the country residencies of Conservative MPs, and no doubt quite a few Labour ones. They tend to live in villages where the relaxed planning regulations, which are threatening to turn Britain into a Monopoly board of second-rate Wendy homes, mysteriously fail to have an effect. That's where to go if you LOVE THE COUNTRYSIDE.

OUR INABILITY TO EXPRESS EMOTION

When Hollywood goes looking for a man to encapsulate the male traits of self-consciousness, bumbling ingratiation and tactful insincerity, they tend not to call on Sylvester Stallone, Bob De Niro or even Ryan Gosling. Nope, they book a flight to London, England, and check in on Hugh, or possibly Colin, or even Daniel (Radcliffe that is, not 'I drink your milkshake' Day-Lewis – he's just weird).

For it is a truth universally acknowledged, that a Hollywood film in possession of an emotionally retarded single male character, must head to these shores, where our public schools, in particular, are the Shaolin temples of charm and reticence development.

Commitment issues? Self-deprecation? Sarcastic one-liners? Stony-faced reaction shots? Acceptance of one's unsatisfactory lot? Yank actors can do one or even two of these at the same time, but it's woven into the fabric of the Brit actor's upbringing – they are the comfort blanket of the British male, of a certain class, from the cradle onwards.

Yep, if you want to Darcy-up a film, come to Britain, where we do emotional constipation by the bucketload – and we do it awfully, awfully well.

OUR OBSESSION WITH THE ROYAL FAMILY

Most countries don't have one. Those that do keep them on a part-time, low-paid basis, where they're expected to chip in and attend events as national representatives, but generally not make a nuisance of themselves and not mind cycling to work.

Not here. In Britain the Royals will be the very last family to All Be In This Together – to suffer the slings and arrows of outrageous austerity. We give them 24/7 funding, half of the countryside and desirable areas of London. They travel everywhere in solid-gold transport, eat and drink only the finest food and wine (and weird ginger biscuits), and go on holiday 200 times a year. On the other hand they host boring dinners, visit boring heads of state and sit through more Annie Lennox performances than is probably safe. It's a strange bargain, but one of those things – like not having revolutions, not having decent public transport, and not winning major sporting tournaments – that we've got so used to that we would panic if presented with the alternative.

Of course, it's quite possible that change may come from within, that we may get our own thoroughly modern family, now that we have young Royals prepared to pose naked for camera-phones and kill people in faraway lands. Well, one of them anyway.

DIY

DO IT YOURSELF has glamorous roots – ruins of a Greek building, dating back to the 6th century BC were uncovered in southern Italy, together with instructions for putting it together (although two stones were critically missing from the diagram). In the 1960s and '70s, a vibrant West Coast scene of American hipsters in San Francisco adopted DIY to reclaim neglected housing stock as part of a wider environmental and convention-breaking movement.

Suburban Britain has managed to dampen down any vestiges of historical excitement possessed by the term DO IT YOURSELF. Instead the words evoke grey Sunday morning journeys in the Austin Allegro, joylessly searching the endless aisles of the local DIY superstore, looking for threaded fasteners with a non-tapered shank, 8 x 4 MDF panels and exterior magnolia emulsion, and returning home for an afternoon of frustrating displacement activity which should hopefully see you through to the onset of evening TV.

Now all that frustration comes flat-packed for your intensified arousal, but there are still two bits missing: the joy and the satisfaction of a day well spent. DIY in Britain is for losers.

THE BBC

Depending on your own particular viewpoint, it's either 'Buggers Broadcasting Communism', or the Establishment's tame media poodle.

The view from abroad, however, is quite often that the BBC is simply the Best Thing About Britain – you know, the one thing foreigners always praise us for. You'd think that something which makes us the envy of the world would make us proud and we'd seek to preserve, strengthen it even. But then that wouldn't be very British would it?

POLITICS

Politics is another area of British life in which class rears its well-coiffured head or doffs its smelly, nicotine-stained cap. As in most other parliaments, politics has long been the preserve of the well bred, well educated and well off. It's only really since the last world war that any semblance of equality of opportunity allowed people from outside that milieu to attempt to enter the Houses of Parliament and shout, 'What about the working classes?' only to be drowned out by a chorus of walrus-like honking from a sea of paper-waving Home Counties oik-bashers.

The language of British politics is at least two-faced, possibly three. Ministers daily attempt the exhausting feat of looking sincerely at their audience with one eye while keeping the other one fixed on media reaction, prepared to reverse their sentiments mid-sentence if it looks propitious to do so. Every speech is littered with sound bites, the magic bullets which are meant to shoot through the radio and TV screen straight into the hearts and minds of the great unwashed, persuading them in an instant of the sincerity and worthiness of the speaker's cause or policy. Yes, they really do think we're that stupid. Hence politics is a profitable resource of British doublespeak for cynical types like ourselves…

❛ LEGACY OF THE LAST GOVERNMENT ❜

'The dire economic situation is a LEGACY OF THE LAST GOVERNMENT, which brought in a range of disastrous measures that we totally agreed with at the time, in fact we didn't think they went anywhere near far enough. However, since coming to power we have seen the effects of these policies to be the total decimation of the country's fiscal health and therefore they are now, officially, to be repeated ad nauseam until every voter in the land cannot help but associate the LAST GOVERNMENT only with this poisonous LEGACY, a LEGACY OF THE LAST GOVERNMENT.'

❛ DIFFICULT DECISIONS ❜

'We have to make difficult decisions if we are to get Britain back on her feet again but, rest assured, these DIFFICULT DECISIONS will not impact personally on me, the Chancellor, or any other member of the cabinet or, to speak frankly if I may, 99.9 per cent of the people I grew up with, know and trust. We will sail through this testing time and avoid the fallout from the DIFFICULT DECISIONS that it falls on me, reluctantly, to make. The impact will explode like a jam roly-poly dropped from the roof of the sports pavilion on the undeserving poor, the feckless and the workshy who, I am persuaded by many of great standing, to be the cause of all our woes and who have been enjoying the high life and living beyond their means for far too long. Some of these undeserving poor have a household pet, such as a Staffordshire bull terrier, and have been feeding it, while claiming they cannot afford to feed their children! Some *of these workshy layabouts have a digital colour television and do very little, I am reliably informed, than sit in front of it all day, smoking and cussing and watching cookery programmes. I ask you, "Have these people inherited wealth?" No. "Do they have trust funds?" No. "Have they been supported through private education and a life of privilege by their hard-working or already independently wealthy parents?" No. Then what gives them the right to be feckless? It is to these people that I now say, the DIFFICULT DECISIONS I have to make are in your own interest. It doesn't matter if you're a confused teenager with a massive skunk habit, a single mother with a disabled child or a 50-something director whose company just went bankrupt, we want to help you back to work by cutting off your benefits, so you must either stack shelves or starve. Because, and I want to be quite clear about this, the private sector is the only way out of this mess, which I may have mentioned is entirely a LEGACY OF THE LAST GOVERNMENT, and by private sector I really mean the supermarkets, the really 'super' markets without which we would be looking at unemployment figures closer to 10 million. The part-time, low-paid insecure jobs offered by these bastions of the British High Street will be available to every one of you now that we've relaxed the planning laws so they can build their superstores on every square inch of this green and pleasant land. Market forces, indeed. Be then assured, if you once again find yourself leading the high life, watching a colour telly, feeding a pet, it will be your own efforts that hoisted you there and well done to you. You are what made Britain Great.'*

❝ WITH THE GREATEST RESPECT ❞

'WITH THE GREATEST RESPECT to the Right Honourable Member sitting opposite, the Socialist Member for Chavington East, who believes that equal education opportunities should be available to all, whose parliamentary researchers all tend to be attractive young women, educated at top public schools, who invariably get a "leg up" of an entirely unexpected nature after a few weeks on the job as it were, who believes fervently that the workers should own the means of production, particularly those workers who designed and installed the handcrafted, bespoke kitchen in his second home using the finest local materials (local to Tuscany, anyway) solely at the taxpayers' expense; who lavishly stocks the aforementioned custom-built kitchen cabinets with the finest wines and foods available in his constituency from delicatessens and superior supermarkets, again exclusively from the taxpayers' purse; and undertakes many research trips across the globe, often in high season, occasionally accompanied by the more eager of his researchers, to determine the damage caused by man-made climate change to the Great Barrier Reef, for instance, or the effects of high fuel prices on tourism in five-star hotels in Bermuda in the winter Parliamentary break, WITH THE GREATEST RESPECT to the Honourable Member he is full of shit – always has been and always will be – and I very much look forward to sharing a massively subsidised bottle of Burgundy with him, and his current intern, after this interminable session of legislation on the minimum wage.'

RADIO FOUR NEWS

'So, Minister, I'm going to ask you a detailed, searching question which will last about 30 seconds of this two-minute interview and which will end with a flourish and a challenge!'

'Well, if I may be permitted to answer that, I'd like to...'

'Ah yes! Exactly, an answer is what we're looking for here, Minister – no prevarication, procrastination or trying to pull us away from the matter in hand'

'No, no, no. As I was about to explain –'

'Well, you'll have to hurry up because we don't have much time left. Let me put a shortened 15-second version of my original question to you, Emphasising The Final Words For Rhetorical Effect. Hmmm?'

'No, the figures quite clearly show –'

'I'm not asking you about the figures, Minister.'

'Actually, er, yes you were, and if I may explain why –'

'Well, yes, we are waiting.'

'Sorry?'

'For an explanation, Minister!'

'But I'm trying to give one and you keep –'

'Sorry, you'll have to do better than that. Now let's take a look at what's coming up later...'

❝ ABSOLUTELY COMMITTED TO ❞

'We are ABSOLUTELY COMMITTED TO promising or saying anything which will get us re-elected or increase our popularity with whoever it is we're trying to impress at any given moment. We will not rest until we have achieved this objective unless we are blown off course by another self-created crisis leading us to reverse all of the measures which, as of this morning, we are ABSOLUTELY COMMITTED TO achieving.'

❝ NOT FIT FOR PURPOSE ❞

'The independent enquiry has found, regrettably, that the Ministry of Truth is NOT FIT FOR PURPOSE. The lack of proper departmental procedures or accounting rigour, and the dysfunctional management structures which are a LEGACY OF THE LAST GOVERNMENT has led to the most damning report on any government department ever published and it's all the previous lot's fault. They themselves, of course, were NOT FIT FOR PURPOSE either.'

❡ WE HAVE BEEN WORKING VERY CLOSELY WITH... ❜

'The Department for Transport is pleased to announce that the number of LEAVES ON THE LINE in the period since the implementation of our landmark 'Leaves Initiative' (The Right Kind of Leaves!) has fallen by almost 50 per cent. WE HAVE BEEN WORKING VERY CLOSELY WITH industry bodies (we want to take all the credit but have to mention them for form's sake) to establish a new paradigm for foliage maintenance and disposal. This has proved to be exceedingly successful and demonstrates how seriously this government takes initiatives of this kind.'

❡ A VISION OF A FUTURE ❜

'I have A VISION OF A FUTURE where British children, incapable of passing our newly rigorous eleven-plus, but unhampered by red tape, bureaucracy and legislation, are encouraged to work in the new hi-tech industries, fracking for gas and cleaning power station chimneys. And, let me be very clear about this, those chimneys will not be emitting high levels of carbon dioxide because the environment is very important to us, as is the health of future generations of our children.'

'THE SQUEEZED MIDDLE'

(Anyone who didn't vote for us last time.)

'HARD-WORKING FAMILIES'

(Anyone who voted for us last time and is now pissed off with us.)

'TRUST ME'

(Vote for me.)

'I CAME INTO POLITICS TO MAKE A DIFFERENCE'

(The difference between having an ordinary job and one with a massive salary and lots of holidays.)

The 'Great' thing about Britain has been our half-hearted, half-arsed approach to everything except beating the Germans. Well, it's good to see that we've remained true to form with our working practices. Having colonised the world with our language, pillaged resources from the Commonwealth and formed a rigidly delineated society where everyone knew their role and their place, at some point it seems we thought we should have a go at this free-market capitalism malarkey, so beloved of our cousins across the Atlantic. Exchanging the gold retirement clock, the brown overalls and the bowler hat – as aspirational symbols of our working life – for bags of coke in the washroom, Ferraris in the garage and mobiles the size of Thanksgiving turkeys, we set about adopting the working practices and jargon of Wall Street. Newsagents, traffic wardens and school dinner ladies were heard chanting 'Greed is Good' as they took down another sucker with a gleam in their eyes.

Now, in the middle of the worst recession ever – brought about entirely by capitalist vultures – we're left with an unholy hotchpotch of balls-out masochistic working hours, second-hand business-guru office philosophies, hand-me-down New York state-of-mind office politics and no resources to make any of it even look like it's working. The good thing about this is it entitles us to a bloody good moan – a very British practice, which was in danger of being eradicated by the relentless positivism of the new office Nazis.

AT THE OFFICE

Offices and working practices have been transformed in recent years by technology and the ruinous global recession. Many more of us eke out a part-time living in a self-styled home office – corner of the living room, kitchen table, bed – in an altruistic attempt to keep down the unemployment statistics, and therefore find our primary means of communication with other human beings to be the deceptively simple business email – deceptive because it is so easy to misjudge the tone and inadvertently cause offence. This accounts for the emergence of those hideous and totally un-British visual punctuations known as 'emoticons' – smiley faces etc. – which litter our communications with paranoid co-workers and distant colleagues, and let them know that we really do love them and find their jokes about the accounts department hilarious and original.

The problem with this arrangement is that it is very one-sided. For the office worker facing the tsunami of email that arrives in their inbox every hour combined with the daily diet of back-to-back meetings, responding to the jokey nudge from the freelancer asking where a contract, payment or offer of work has got to, is often a task left to fester for weeks on end. Meanwhile the freelancer sitting alone in a chilly home conjures up all sorts of paranoid scenarios, all of which end with no work ever again; and of course, in a very British way, allowing the resentment and bitterness to generate a lake of bile.

For those lucky souls who have remained gainfully employed at a location other than their own home, there is the joy of 'meetings' – joyful gatherings of office staff, which are generally a very good way to waste time discussing matters that could have been resolved in a simple phone call in a twentieth of the time. They are a great opportunity

To: ----
CC: ----
From: ----
Subject: This Morning's Meeting

Hi all,

Thanks for your time this morning – A VERY PRODUCTIVE MEETING I felt. Gary, your idea about increasing the frequency of our meetings was brilliant, though I agree, Steve, that we urgently need to review the in-house snack provision so we avoid getting caught short of muffins and coffee – essential boosts for meetings extending over the hour. Perhaps we could meet this afternoon to talk through the options? Can we leave it to you, Dave, to reschedule and agree the date of the next three weekly meetings, due to the upcoming company conferences?

I've got meetings every day this week so perhaps we should pencil in a meet to review these conclusions from what was, as I have already stated, A VERY PRODUCTIVE MEETING this morning.

All best,

Harry

'A VERY PRODUCTIVE MEETING'

for the self-promoting, the control freak and the otherwise too-easy-to-get-away-from droning office bore to practise their office superpowers on you, until you are driven to contemplate how easy it would be to commit suicide, or murder, with a paperclip.

❛ LEAVE IT WITH ME ❜

'That's a really great suggestion which requires quite a lot of thought. Thanks. Could you LEAVE IT WITH ME so I can mull it over? (I'll get back to you as soon as the grass becomes a bit longer and I can kick your completely insane – sorry, inspiring – idea into it.)'

SACKED

As discussed elsewhere (see ROAD RAGE, p.52), we aren't particularly disposed to confront anyone about anything if we can avoid it. Therefore when the moment comes for an employee to be relieved of his corporate electronic tag (sorry, Blackberry) the scene more often than not looks like an awkward relationship break-up conversation than two professionals (well, one soon-to-be ex-professional) discussing the end of a contract. Blame-free phrases are gently exchanged which will resonate with all of us who have been through a break-up…

CORPORATE	PERSONAL
It hasn't quite worked out the way we hoped.	It's not working for me.
Sorry, but we're going to have to let you go.	I'm sorry but I think it's better if we split up.
Thank you for all your hard work but...	You're a lovely bloke but...
Could you hand back the Blackberry?	Would you delete those pictures we took in Spain?
We're not sure that you find the work challenging enough.	It's not you, it's me.
I'm sure you'll find another position quickly.	You can do so much better than me.

...and if you do get the sack, you're going to need a reference, where the art of not quite saying what you mean (as in the famous 'If you can get this man to work for you, you will be very lucky') has reached an estimable degree of sophistication.

CORPORATE COMMUNICATIONS

When the Wall Street-ese of CORPORATE COMMUNICATIONS started to pour out of the fax machine in the early 1990s, few would have thought that we Brits would embrace this language so wholeheartedly. But we have and, as it turns out, we're rather good at it. The reason for this is that it saves everyone the embarrassment of saying anything in plain and forthright terms. Just as our diplomats were considered wily magicians of obfuscation and doublethink, we have taken up business gobbledygook with a similarly impressive aptitude for using a lot of words without actually saying anything…

To: ----
CC: ----
From: ----

Hi Sarah,

DID YOU GET MY LAST EMAIL? Just checking that it didn't end up in your Spam box or that IT had managed to lose yet another one! LOL. Just wanted to check in with you about my idea – I think it has legs. Would love to hear your view. I'm around: text, phone (mobile, landline), email, Facebook, LinkedIn, smoke signals (joke!) – get hold of me any way you want. I'm around most of the rest of the day and most of the week. In fact I'm not doing anything but waiting for you to get in touch.

Looking forward to hearing from you soon (IT department permitting!).

Jonathan

'DID YOU GET MY LAST EMAIL?'

To: ----
CC: ----
From: ----

Hi Steve,

Hope you're well and that you liked the designs[1]. I was just wondering when the invoice I submitted six weeks ago might be paid? I realise you are incredibly busy[2] but would appreciate it if you could ask the accounts department for me[3]. Would be great to catch up with you at some point[4] very soon.

All best,

Brian

1. I sent them two months ago on the agreed deadline but haven't heard anything from you
2. Unlike me, sitting at home wondering when the next job is coming from
3. I haven't turned the heating on all winter and am eking out the last of the baked beans to survive
4. Please buy me a drink or something to eat and at least give me the hope of some more work

'DO YOU KNOW WHEN MY INVOICE MIGHT BE PAID?'

❛ ...IS PROUD TO ANNOUNCE ❜ ·

'Innovative market leaders[1] in mohair technology, Ibex Global today IS PROUD TO ANNOUNCE the launch of a cutting-edge[2] new product from our uniquely talented[3] sustainability[4] team. Ibex continually strives[5] to set the standards for modern mohair technology and to ensure that the industry adds value[6] to the UK's booming animal-hair export industry. This new product[7] changes the face of the mohair industry once again[8].'

1. Nobody else is stupid enough to do it
2. Well, it was when we thought of it two years ago
3. Unemployable anywhere else
4. Recycling old ideas
5. In press releases
6. And we get tax breaks
7. Insert stupid acronym here
8. And we hope it makes some money or all of our uniquely talented –
see above – team are fucked

❛ HEALTH AND SAFETY GONE MAD ❜

'Thank God this government is showing some sense about HEALTH AND SAFETY. I mean that last lot, you couldn't make a cup of tea without having to get a criminal-record check and a form signed in triplicate from your doctor and a social worker – HEALTH AND SAFETY GONE MAD, I tell you. And you'd have to go on a two-day course just to learn how to move a ladder. Now, if you accidentally spray hydrochloric acid over your co-workers, who aren't wearing protective clothing, because you're

falling backwards off a ladder, which was leaning in the wrong place when the forklift nudged it sideways, then you'll only have yourself to blame, because you didn't use any common sense.'

TRADES

TRADES used to be something we took a pride in here in Britain, or so legend has it. A fantasy world of hardware stores, brown coats, pencils behind ears and spirit levels once existed, apparently, like a Middle Earth of manual occupation. Now it seems like we invite apprentice plumbers to spliff their way through a two-week college course before being let loose to recreate the last hours of the *Titanic* in your upstairs bathroom, or charging you the GDP of a small African nation to fiddle, unsuccessfully, with your boiler.

It's no surprise that an army of well-trained, polite, industrious army of East European tradespeople has invaded Britain, bringing their controversial characteristics of hard work, fair prices and quality workmanship to marble-topped tables up and down the land.

At least we can still rely on estate agents to provide the ineptitude, overcharging and downright incompetence which we Brits have come to expect from our 'tradespeople'.

'Nie podoba mi si, ze wygląd'

'Nie podoba mi się wygląd that Damp to jest? OK niech okiem – Prawo Ja po prostu wyciągnąć to – oh – NIE PODOBA MI SIĘ, ŻE WYGLĄD, że – co masz tam jest przepalony tynku. Nie jest to dobry znak. Miałem nadzieję, że nie znajdzie tego. Widzisz, gdy woda dostaje się i uzyskać w nim będzie, to musi gdzieś iść, w twoim przypadku to będzie wszędzie. Naprawdę nie lubię patrzeć na to. Widzisz, kiedy notowane do tej pracy, to na tej podstawie, że zgodziliśmy się, co było podstawą, ponieważ nie stwierdził.'

'I don't like the look of that'

'Damp is it? OK, let's have a look – right, I'll just pull this – oh – I DON'T LIKE THE LOOK OF THAT – what you've got there is blown plaster. Not a good sign. I was hoping we wouldn't find that. You see, when water gets in, and get in it will, it has to go somewhere, and in your case it's going everywhere. I really do not like the look of that. You see, when I quoted for this job, it was on the basis that we agreed, which was the basis of not finding that.'

CONSULTANTS

We Brits are suckers for professionals telling us what to do, regardless of their efficacy. We revere our doctors, venerate our lawyers, and even respect our chief constables – perhaps it's an authority–inferiority complex – but anyway, we don't tend to have revolutions or civil wars, unlike the rest of the planet. Yes, we are all in awe of professionals, which explains the peculiarly British phenomenon of the CONSULTANT.

Consultant (*n*). A 'professional' who provides useless, long-winded advice in exchange for extortionate sums of money.

'The bank balance is looking healthy and we have a good reputation. We'd better get a CONSULTANT in to change our brand with a misrepresentative, meaningless renaming, and charge us a fortune. That way we can subsequently hire another CONSULTANT and pay them massive wonga to tell us to revert to our original identity.'
'Good idea.'

Note: CONSULTANTS are particularly good at fucking up national companies, public services and government departments, but they will have a go at anything if the price is right.

PROPERTY DETAILS

13 Shitside Close
Merrydown
Sorrey
£900,000
3-bedroom semi-detached house

This magnificent[1] Victorian terraced property, in the up-and-coming[2] suburb of Merrydown, is in need of some TLC[3] but offers a wealth of features[4] to the lucky buyer[5].

Deceptively spacious[6], it is comprised of two reception rooms[7], three bedrooms including two double bedrooms with en-suite bathrooms[8], and a kitchen-diner[9].

A delightful, compact[10] garden offers superb views of the surrounding countryside[11]. The property is situated close to all local amenities[12] and within the sought-after[13] Merrydown High School catchment area. Well-situated for local transport routes[14]. Early viewing recommended[15].

No onward chain[16].

1. Available
2. Urban ghetto
3. A total disaster – take the asking price and double it for renovations
4. A ropey fireplace and cornicing – and rising damp
5. Desperate sucker
6. Tiny
7. A small living room and an eat-off-your-lap-because-you-ain't-getting-a-table-in-here dining room
8. For intimately sharing the odour of waste throughout the night with a loved one
9. See reception rooms
10. Think tiny then halve it
11. The neighbours' back gardens
12. There's a supermarket on the ring road a stone's throw away
13. Pupils often 'sought-after' by the police
14. Between a motorway and a ring road – 24/7 traffic guaranteed
15. I need this sale to get next month's sales bonus
16. No one else would touch it with a barge pole

TRAVEL,
WEATHER
& ABROAD

Roads, railways and airports are a constant source of misery and, therefore, pleasure for the British. Whereas we marvel at well-maintained autobahns, traffic-free autoroutes, precise arrivals at Swiss platforms and the 24-hour operation of some New York subway stations, one senses relief that none of our transport systems offer such comfort, efficiency or cohesion. Well, at least among those who don't have to use them every day.

The merest fluctuation in our climate – a butterfly flapping its soggy wings in Chipping Sodbury, for example – has a grotesquely disproportionate effect on the efficiency of our highways. One millimetre of rain above the seasonal average is likely to bring our railways to a halt. A single Celsius drop on the thermometer can cause chaos on our roads.

But that's OK because it gives us something to talk about – or rather a conduit, to express the whole gamut of human emotions without for a moment giving the impression that we might be responsible for these feelings or, indeed, attach responsibility for them to someone else's actions.

Many other books have been written about the behaviour of the British when they set foot on warm, foreign soil, so don't worry, we have no intention of delaying you with a detailed study. Instead we've provided an *amuse-bouche* of observations to get you in the mood for your next great escape.

❝ LEAVES ON THE LINE ❞

'Virgin Trains apologises for the cancellation of the 16:15 service from Liverpool Lime Street to London Euston. The track has been temporarily incapacitated by LEAVES ON THE LINE. We would like to extend our sincere regrets to all those passengers who had hoped to travel using our trains today on their hugely expensive pre-booked seats. Instead, please feel free to lay siege to the next available service and see if you can squeeze yourself into a space next to the overflowing toilets.'

❝ WRONG KIND OF LEAVES ❞

'First Great Western is sorry to have to announce severe delays in the service from Exeter to Plymouth. This is due to the WRONG KIND OF LEAVES falling onto the track. Health and Safety executives and qualified rail sweepers are racing to the scene of the problem as we speak and our normal service will be resumed as soon as possible. In the meantime First Great Western encourage passengers who are experiencing this inconvenience to spend some money in the overpriced snack bar on the platform, which provides a wide range of obesity-inducing snacks.'

THE BUFFET CAR

'A wide range of food and beverages freshly prepared (microwaved) by our on-board catering technicians is available in THE BUFFET CAR. The menu includes paninis (cardboard – fillings indeterminate), fresh fruit (at prices that make Harrods look like a food bank) and hot and cold drinks including wine (in plastic bottles with a bouquet of tin and acrylic), continental beers (bottled in South Wales with free yeast infection thrown in) and tea and coffee (molten hot and yet tasteless – like drinking boiled battery acid). Our trained staff (they have been taught how to put on plastic gloves) look forward to serving you (in between driving the train, collecting the tickets, cleaning the toilets – well, they are being paid a living wage) for the duration of your journey with us today (and quite possibly tomorrow unless the mess at Crewe is sorted in the next six hours).'

❛ WE ARE CURRENTLY EXPERIENCING MINOR DELAYS ❜

'London Underground apologise to customers as WE ARE CURRENTLY EXPERIENCING MINOR DELAYS on the District Line (you might see a train in the next 30 minutes or so). This is due to the late running (there was never a hope of finishing on schedule – everyone was being paid overtime) of planned (for maximum disruption) engineering works (changing some light bulbs). There are also similar MINOR DELAYS on the Piccadilly, Northern and Metropolitan Lines; otherwise there is a good service on all other routes (slow to snail-paced – apart from the

Circle Line, which is always completely fucked so we don't bother mentioning it).'

RESIDENTIAL PARKING SCHEME

The RESIDENTIAL PARKING SCHEME (RPS) is an anti-travel ruse dreamed up by local government (and no doubt CONSULTANTS) which has the added benefit of being able to charge people for something they already had for free. An RPS is usually introduced after a 'consultation' – which is government doublespeak for pretending to listen and then going right ahead and doing what they had planned to all along (for example SUPERMARKETS, see p.127), housing developments and pretty much any controversial policy which is to be dumped on a horrified community).

Once the local authority hasn't got the agreement of the community, it starts to charge them for the right to park outside their own homes, and to prevent them parking in neighbouring residential zones without a guest permit (which they flog like prizeless lottery tickets to the meek and angry).

Businesses and residents alike rejoice at being given an exclusive right to park on their own street at precisely the time of day that most of them won't be there, preventing harassed and extorted commuters and tourists from making use of the space, leading to the cattle-market transportation conditions commonly enjoyed on British public transport (except no cow has ever paid £4,000 a year for the privilege of going to town) and depriving local businesses of valuable daytime customers.

By night, most schemes are relaxed, allowing residents to park outside their own homes, and invite their out-of-zone friends to do so, providing they have a voucher prominently displayed, correctly filled in and not past its sell-by date. Urban Brits have been known to wander the streets of foreign cities for hours, marvelling at the free and plentiful parking, keeping a wary lookout for ticket machines and zombified armies of RPS enforcement officers patrolling the kerbs, such is the bovine conditioning foisted upon us at home in order to raise yet another stealth tax. 'Welcome to Britain!' the RPS screams – 'Though not between the hours of 8am to 6pm Monday to Friday, Weekends or Bank Holidays!'

❮ WE ARE NOW PRIORITY BOARDING ❯

'We shall be PRIORITY BOARDING rows 1–12 in a moment, so the self satisfied retirees clutching their complimentary orange juice that cost them £15, and their free copy of yesterday's Express, *can smirk as you locate your cramp-inducing child's seat while they stretch their ample 5-foot-3 frames into the extra-leg-room space they've paid more than an arm and a leg for.'*

ROAD RAGE

Although by no means a mode of behaviour limited to, or originating from, the roads of Britain, there is something intrinsically British about ROAD RAGE. Maybe it's the opportunity to show seething pent-up aggression from a safe distance, or the fact that our roads are so congested, like arterial blood encountering a blockage and inducing traffic heart seizures, but we've taken to it like psychotic ducks to boiling water.

Which of us hasn't experienced the pleasure of an idiot in an Audi inserting his headlights into your bumper while gesturing wildly in your rear-view mirror and talking loudly to the office on his mobile? Who hasn't witnessed the most mild-mannered Micra driver turn into a frothy-mouthed, apoplectic speed freak when stuck behind an oblivious older couple doing 21mph in a 30-zone?

Thankfully the RAGE rarely develops into physical confrontation – so maybe it could be viewed in a positive light, as an opportunity to safely let off steam and relieve ourselves of the tension of being constantly British, if only for a minute or two. Whichever way you look at it, ROAD RAGE has become as British as, and much more common than, the BOBBIES ON THE BEAT (see p.14).

THE WEATHER

The weather – more British than cups of tea and cucumber sandwiches with the Queen.

Samuel Johnson, the poet and lexicographer, observed in 1758, 'When two Englishmen meet, their first talk is of the weather.' And in the eyes of the world, nothing defines us more clearly than the suffering inflicted on us by our island geography and the doughty manner in which we turn that pain into the glue which holds us together – or at least holds together the conversations we have with everyone from our closest friends and family to the strangers we must tolerate for the sake of appearances. A recent survey estimated that Britons spend an average of six months of their lives talking about the weather. That is to say, we talk about it quite a lot, often to people we don't know very well – which makes it worth remarking on.

We never have anything particularly interesting to say about it, but that's OK. Talking about the weather is generally just another way of saying 'Hello' or 'I don't hate you'. Of course, this being Britain, there are occasions when weatherspeak may be deployed as a form of one-upmanship – 'Looks like it's been rainy down your way; we've had brilliant sunshine here' – but generally the tone is non-aggressive. Neutral ground is being sought to express conviviality.

It's quite extraordinary, though, the impact that such a mild, grey climate has on our society. The fact that we still talk in awed tones about the Great Storm of 1987 – no stronger than the yearly hurricanes which batter the coasts of the US – show what a pushover we are for a bit of wind and rain. Snow falling in England for five days in a row brings the country to its knees. Anything veering more than a few degrees away from the year-round norm has us reaching for the record books and stockpiling tuna chunks in brine.

FORECASTING THE WEATHER

What is said:
'A warm front moving in from the south should bring above average temperatures for June.'

What is meant:
'It's going to hit 20 degrees Celsius for approximately three minutes around lunchtime. Rain should be back with us by 2pm.'

What is said:
'And it looks like the good weather should be with us for a while longer, as that warm front pushes in from over the Atlantic.'

What is meant:
'It's going to hit 20 degrees Celsius for approximately three minutes around lunchtime. Rain should be back with us by 2pm.'

What is said:
'Rain should be with us by lunchtime, heavy at times and falling on already sodden ground.'

What is meant:
'Get the lifeboats out, start swimming, but don't forget to take details of your insurance policy in a waterproof pouch.'

What is said:
'We can expect a smattering of snow throughout the South-east, which should turn to slush by the morning.'

What is meant:
'Got a meeting tomorrow? Need to take a train or a plane? Forget it, even though they're coping with 2 feet of snow and ice throughout the Continent.'

What is said:
'We'll have some wintry conditions over the course of the next week.'

What is meant:
'There's a possibility of snow or heavy rainfall and it'll be cold but, sadly, none of these will be severe enough to allow you to bunk off work or school for the day.'

NICE WEATHER WE'RE HAVING

A: 'MORNING. NICE WEATHER WE'RE HAVING.'

('I really can't think of anything I want to say to you.')

B: 'YES, ISN'T IT. MEANT TO BE RAINING LATER.'

('Neither can I. Can I go now?')

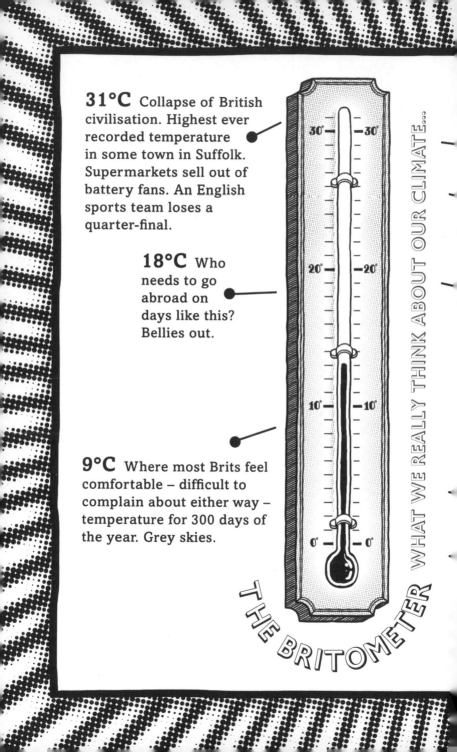

31°C Collapse of British civilisation. Highest ever recorded temperature in some town in Suffolk. Supermarkets sell out of battery fans. An English sports team loses a quarter-final.

18°C Who needs to go abroad on days like this? Bellies out.

9°C Where most Brits feel comfortable – difficult to complain about either way – temperature for 300 days of the year. Grey skies.

WHAT WE REALLY THINK ABOUT OUR CLIMATE...

THE BRITOMETER

30°C Droughts, pestilence, people dying from heat exhaustion, global warming hits the headlines.

25°C 'It's too hot.' Major complaints about air-conditioning in offices. Office workers near windows fan faces and roll eyes in disbelief at temperature.

20°C Balmy summer's day (with showers). Tragically unsuitable summer gear in evidence everywhere.

10°C Unseasonably warm winter's day.

5°C T-shirts and shorts weather in Newcastle. If accompanied by sunshine, in February, millions of gardeners will emerge and plant seeds, which will be killed by frost two days later.

0°C Major disruption: airports closed; railways unusable; tobogganing on 10-inch strips of ice covered in dog shit.

TRAVELLING ABROAD

When we go 'abroad', we have a tendency to either to go with utter suspicion of everything and everyone, or with the feeling that everything is so superior – the food, the climate, the culture – that we should spend our time dumbstruck, in awe at all we behold (and ignore the virulent racism, misogyny, skin cancer and ghastly music that one is just as likely to encounter in reality).

The truth – *quelle surprise!* – generally lies somewhere *au milieu* (maybe not so much in North Korea). All other countries have their good points and bad points, just like Britain.

FOREIGN GREETINGS WE HAVE NOT QUITE MASTERED

Ça va?
(Um, please don't answer with anything longer than '*ça va?*')

Hola!
(Um, please don't answer…)

Ciao!
(Um…)

It's more a question of looking to have our expectations, or prejudices, verified or confirmed.

Of course, it doesn't help when we're visiting a place where the language is foreign to us or, even worse, where the population has forgotten to learn fluent English. This is why we may appear more at home somewhere like the US (apart from the prospect of being shot or asked to have a nice day – both appalling prospects for the average Brit) or Australia (see racism, misogyny etc.).

Yes, when our birthright, our beloved language, is placed on shaky grounds, strange things happen to it, and us…

STAG AND HEN PARTIES

There are few more chilling sights to the sane British tourist than a group of young British women, scantily dressed in neon pink or luminous red with dildoes strapped to their chest and L-plates pinned like a tar-and-feathering to the poor cow who's actually getting married – perhaps a similarly clad group of young British men? Anyway, to see such a group trollied at 3 o'clock in the afternoon in the middle of a beautiful medieval city like Prague or Sofia (or wherever's the current cheapest destination on the Easyair conveyor belt of inebriated 20-somethings destined to ruin our reputation abroad), is to realise that so-called budget travel has its downsides.

ON THE MENU

What the average Brit abroad thinks when he sees…

Prix fixe: 'They've fixed the prices – let's go somewhere else'
A la carte: 'Anything off the trolley'
Tapas: 'Not full English – avoid'
Meze: See 'Tapas'
Carafe: 'Glass'
Litre: 'Big glass'
Carpaccio: 'Fish, I expect'
Frutti di mare : 'Horse manure?… avoid'
Antipasti Misto: 'Not pasta – probably in steam… avoid'
Pizza: 'Italian full English – result'
Bolognese: See 'Pizza'

SHOUT, SHOUT, LET IT ALL OUT

Instead of learning some phrases before you go on holiday, practise shouting your questions in English, as this will usually help the ignorant, befuddled, lazy waiter understand your request: 'DO YOU HAVE A TABLE FOR TWO?' (*'Avez-vous une table pour deux?'*), for example.

This technique works well outside the restaurant too, in almost any situation. At the market, instead of inquiring,

'*Dónde puedo encontrar salchichas inglesas?*' just holler, 'WHERE CAN I FIND SOME ENGLISH SAUSAGES?' At the nightclub, instead of explaining, '*Lo siento – mi novio acaba de ser enfermo en su bolso de mano,*' yell, 'SORRY – MY BOYFRIEND HAS JUST BEEN SICK IN YOUR HANDBAG!' They're bound to come around to your style of communication and if they don't at first, try using the international language of your hands to gesture your meaning.

FAKE TAN

As is well known in Britain, a tan (or, to be more accurate, a FAKE TAN) comes out of a bottle. The result is meant to imitate the effect of overexposure to something called 'The Sun' (the warming, life-giving one, not the tabloid rag) which we Brits glimpse occasionally, like some long-heralded comet, between the months of May and September. The effect can also be duplicated by going on holiday and shouting loudly at the sky. The bottle option is cheaper, if not nearly so much fun.

A FAKE TAN is meant to imbue the wearer with the healthy appearance of someone who spends their life gallivanting around California, surfing or riding a BMX bike. Pity, then, that it usually makes the tan-ee look like they got caught in the crossfire in the spraying booth of a car factory, or in the way of their dad painting the garden fence.

When you think about it, FAKE TANNING is quite a weird thing to do – you don't see that many fake melanomas, after all – which makes it a perfectly British preoccupation.

Sport in Britain was the preserve of the gentlemen class until the last century or so – not that you'd guess from the behaviour of modern-day sportsmen and women who twist the concept of 'sporting behaviour' inside out and upside down to achieve victory. And nowhere is this more blatant than in professional football.

Diving, time-wasting, insulting the referee's ex-wife, pretending to have been tortured by the Taliban – they'll do anything to steal a point or inflict a disadvantage on an opponent.

British footie stars have a fascinating line in doublespeak. These psychotically driven unhinged professionals, who would manufacture and sell essence of their own grandparents for a competitive edge during a 'game', turn into self-effacing, balanced analysts in the contractually obligated post-match interview. Unlike in other countries, there is an unacknowledged requirement for answers to be seasoned with a noticeable measure of British self-deprecation – this is generally how we Brits like our sports fodder.

SPORTS COMMENTARY

Sporting commentary is an excellent opportunity to observe those British traits of understatement, complaining, cynicism and fault-finding working at full pelt. Not for us the never-ending South American 'Gooooaaaaaaallllllllllll!' celebrations, or blatant Australian nationalism. Oh, no: we prefer the relentless anticipation of defeat and ignominy – even a scoreline of 5-0 up with ten minutes to go can only provoke doom-laden questions like 'They can't surely throw it away from this position, can they?' British commentators take pessimism and turn it into an art form.

'I CAN'T **BELIEVE** WHAT I'M SEEING OUT THERE TODAY'

('Although it's exactly the same as I saw last week and I'll see every week until I retire.')

'THIS IS **JUST** UNBELIEVABLE'

('I'm making a 0-0 draw between Sunderland and Wigan sound like Wagner's bloody Ring Cycle – no, not the one off X Factor.')

'THE ODDS ARE STACKED **AGAINST** THEM'

('There's more chance of Save the Children giving out Jimmy Savile masks that this lot winning.')

THE MANAGER'S POST-MATCH INTERVIEW

'He's a great advert for the game'

(He earns £200,000 a week, has five children by five different mothers, has been arrested twice for 'nightclub incidents', and once for letting off fireworks in Harrods, but he hasn't been sent off yet or been caught taking drugs.')

'We need to improve our zonal marking'

('We were running around like headless chickens while they scored at will.')

'Having so many attacking options is a nice problem to have'

('It's a complete managerial nightmare – egos the size of an oligarch's wallet and all of them with the ability to sulk like a 5-year-old.')

'Their centre-forward went down rather easily'

('He fell over like he'd been shot in the legs, back and head in spite of the fact a CSI investigation would be hard-pressed to find any trace of physical contact. He is without doubt a cheating bastard.')

'WE'RE TAKING EACH GAME AS IT COMES'

('We've won two games in a row – fuck knows how.')

'WE WERE THE BETTER TEAM IN THE FIRST HALF'

('We went in 2-0 down at half-time, which was better than the final 7-1 scoreline.')

'HE'S BEEN SUFFERING A LACK OF CONFIDENCE IN FRONT OF GOAL'

('The only way he'd score at the moment would be an OWN goal if he was IN goal.')

'HE'S NOT QUITE MATCH FIT BUT HE'S GETTING THERE'

('He got straight on the coach from a three-day bender but he did puke up several times on the way to the ground.')

THE PLAYER'S POST-MATCH INTERVIEW

'We're too good to go down'
('The team's full of ageing, overpaid prima donnas who can't stand each other and will leave the club as soon as it's relegated.')

'On days like this it's not about the money'
('I just got paid what you might earn in five years for running around for 90 minutes – hang on, I'd better take this call from my agent.')

'There are no easy games at this level'
('We've just lost an international to a team containing a part-time postman, a baker and a farmer. And his dog. His blind, three-legged dog.')

'I'm not going anywhere – we're in talks about a new contract'
'My agent is in talks about a new contract ith anyone who will double my wages.')

'We were very well organised'
('We didn't stray outside our own half and kicked the shit out of anything in a different-coloured top.')

'It was a physical battle, but then football is a contact sport'
('I gave him several, sneaky icks in the plum hammock.')

'WE ALWAYS KNEW IT WAS GOING TO BE TOUGH'

('...especially after the fifteenth pint of lager at 3 o'clock this morning.')

'WE FEEL A LITTLE HARD DONE-BY'

('The ref was in the pocket of the opposition – no doubt he's driving out of the ground in a brand-new Bentley.')

PETS

Nothing sets us Brits apart from our fellow humans more than our uncompromising love of animals – particularly of the domesticated variety. Britain was the first country to introduce hairy-friend welfare legislation and over 50 per cent of families keep a pet in the home (as well as a university graduate). Over on the Continent, where they would sooner drop a donkey from a tenth-floor window than take a pet for a pedicure, they think we're totally bonkers.

And they could well be right. A recent survey showed that, while the majority of consumers were cutting back on all purchases, welding shut wallets and generally watching their lives grind to a halt in the face of the worst recession ever, animal lovers were refusing to scrimp on luxury pet food and other animal treats – preferring to starve themselves or their children if needs be, so that Tiddles can loll around all day with the central heating on; still, at least that might stop it from murdering Britain's wildlife or shitting in next-door's garden.

So deep is our affection for our dumb friends, that you can buy almost anything you might treat yourself to when feeling flush, in spite of the fact your pet won't have a clue what's going on: exotic facials, designer clothes, hypnotherapy, four-poster pet beds, dog beers, pupcakes (cupcakes for dogs) – you think of it, in Britain, someone will sell it to you.

SLYTHERIN

While cats and dogs steal the limelight and are pretty much guaranteed to fight it out for Britain's Favourite Pet status each year, there is a huge underclass of creatures that have been adopted, and adapted, to the social mores of these isles. We're talking reptiles.

The British have a fascination with scaly beasts – especially snakes, which we fear beyond all reason, perhaps because our only indigenous, venomous creature is the adder – the Lord Lucan of the reptile world. If you're bitten by an adder you should be Britain's official entry in the World Bad Luck Championships, such is their rarity and elusiveness.

But yes, there is something about the slithering, hiss and slink of a snake, in particular, which draws us hypnotised to overheated pet shops where we may purchase for young Luke a vivarium, a bag of frozen mice, and a boa constrictor optimistically named 'Kuddles' – destined to panic the neighbours when he goes AWOL for 48 hours, before being found wrapped round the exhaust pipe of a nearby Honda Civic.

Local newspapers love pet shops and snakes, because when they go missing (and they always go missing), snakes are perfect headline fodder – 'Have you seen Monty's Python?'; 'Snakes On Ash Lane' – and add a touch of the exotic to the usual diet of supermarket openings, road accidents and bus timetable chaos.

STUPID THINGS DOG OWNERS SAY

'He's very friendly'
(Despite having had his balls chopped off he'll still mount any passing object – including, sorry, your leg.)

'She's quite playful'
(Oh look, she's swinging your dog around by the throat! Little minx!')

'He can be a little boisterous'
(You'd better put this chainmail on.)

'He's all right when he gets to know you'
(But he'll have killed you by then, unfortunately.)

WHAT CATS
REALLY THINK OF
THEIR OWNERS

'She's so intelligent – she can tell what I'm thinking'
(Cat: 'I'm with stupid'.)

'He scratches me and sprays on my bed, but it's just a sign of affection'
(Cat: 'I despise you; Jeez, what do I have to do to get this through to you? Now go and get me some food.')

'She's brought me a present!'
(Cat: 'I've eviscerated some neighbourhood vermin because I was bored. Now turn the heating up and fuck off.')

BRITISH PETS
LOOKING FOR...

Unpredictable pit bull terrier WLTM shifty, drug-dealing male, mid-20s, with view to intimidating alliance. Pref. inner city.

Highly strung Siamese, looking for high-maintenance couple, into the performing arts and showing off.

Preening Chihuahua seeks minor celebrity's handbag for mutual publicity opportunities. Must have good PA for rest-of-life needs. One-year contract.

Inexhaustible Cocker Spaniel seeks naïve middle-class couple for long country walks – ideally three or four per day followed by lots of ROFL.

Tinkerbell, **beautiful mare pony**, seeks precocious 7-year-old for novice show-jumping, tears before bedtime and growing disinterest. Own paddock essential.

Goldfish seeks escape from plastic bag at fairground hell. Any reasonable offers considered! Goldfish seeks escape from plastic bag at fairground hell. Any reasonable offers considered! Goldfish…

WHAT PEOPLE SAY TO THEIR CHILDREN WHEN THEIR PET DIES

'We had to put Aslan to sleep – he was old and in pain and couldn't stop going to the toilet'
(Does that mean we're putting granddad to sleep too, Mummy?)

'Felix has gone to a big scratching post in the sky, where he can roll and pounce and scratch all day'
(If I jump under Daddy's car, will I get there too?)

WHAT KIND OF PET OWNER WOULD YOU MAKE?

1. Your son's hamster needs an operation that will necessitate remortgaging your home. Do you?

a) Contact the building society first thing in the morning.

b) Explain to your son that if Peanut's cataracts are to be removed, you'll have to use school fees and he'll have to go to comprehensive school next term.

c) Flush Peanut down the loo, and tell your son that he's gone on a Gap Year holiday, like his older sister.

2. You've run out of cat food and friends have just arrived for a special dinner. Do you?

a) Cut up the beef tournedos and feed them to the cat, give your guests vegetables and explain that you're fasting this week. Being British they will, of course, agree.

b) Ignore the plaintive wailing of your hungry cat and shove her in the garden to get her own dinner for once. That's what they used to be for, right?

c) Stuff a sock in Sookie's mouth and lock her in a kitchen cupboard. She can have scraps later.

3. You're looking after your neighbour's dog while they're on holiday. It wants to play 'fetch' incessantly. Do you?

a) Spend hours throwing a ball and relishing Biggles' joy as he faithfully returns it to you within seconds.

b) Throw it a couple of times and then ignore the whimpering hound and his big brown, watery eyes.

c) Throw the ball into the road 'by mistake'. Never could stand that dog.

Mostly a) – Congratulations. You are almost certainly a British pet owner. Your animal has won the Pet Lottery!

Mostly b) – Hmmm. Are you a sociopath? Do you really like other creatures? Pets have feelings too, you know.

Mostly c) – Are you sure you're not Spanish or something?

Like many other areas of British life and language, how you raise your children depends to a large extent on how you were brought up yourself and how you see yourself in relation to the rest of British society.

Although the approach of all classes to parenting has changed in the last 50 years, it's fair to say that the greatest changes have been seen in the reliably neurotic middle classes, where parenting in Britain has swung from sadism to masochism in little more than a generation.

The middle classes are desperate to both maintain the gap between themselves and the Great Unwashed (who nevertheless are encroaching on their catchment areas with their White Van incomes) and stay within mimicking distance of the entitled upper classes.

A perplexing proliferation of childrearing advice, together with an urge to 'engage' with their offspring in a way their parents never did with them, has left the contemporary middle-class adult bereft of the certainties that instructed their development.

Meanwhile another great tradition of British parenting is also flourishing: parental absenteeism. Offloading children to boarding schools or, er, state-run residential institutions remains a reliable way of getting others to bring up your children in a traditional British way.

LEARNING ENVIRONMENTS

School and education in general can be a testing place for the English language. Up until the 1980s, it was perfectly acceptable for teachers to put the boot into their charges' lack of attainment and to be straightforward about what they expected pupils to do. Nowadays, teachers are instructed to 'focus' on the positives and blunt any hint of sharp criticism with a bewildering phrase book of pseudo-business speak that hides any actual meaning. Pupils have become 'learners' or even 'stakeholders', headteachers 'leaders', teachers 'classroom practitioners'; lessons must have 'closure' and there are 'baseline assessments' before pupils – sorry, 'learners' – embark on their 'learning journeys'. And it's not just teachers: journalists, politicians, and bureaucrats – anyone, in fact, involved in the educational circus – all succumb to this non-language. Add to the buzzword babble our own innate ability to obfuscate and dress thoughts up in euphemism and the result is that the language of British education is about as clear as the instruction manual for the Large Hadron Collider.

In spite of the intrusion of this half-baked business terminology, the underlying trends haven't really changed that much: some pupils are brighter than others, some parents are richer than others, and some teachers 'could try harder' than others.

SCHOOL REPORT CARDS

NB – The key word in any report is 'sometimes', which actually means 'constantly'.

ENGLISH - 6C
Noah shows some promise in his learning activities but sometimes a lack of focus in the stakeholder environment hampers the full realisation of his expressive potential. (He's the person who instigates the riots each lesson.)

MATHS - 5A
Emily has undoubted aptitude in number-based learning but sometimes she misses out on her learning outcome targets because of a focus shortfall. (Could try harder.)

SCIENCE - 5C
Oliver's home-based learning options are sometimes proving to be quite a challenge for him but otherwise his progress in science is steady. (Never does his homework, haven't noticed him at all in class.)

HISTORY - 4A
Jack has all the tools he needs to become an excellent historian (I think he can read) and has often (opposite of 'sometimes', means 'rarely') made valuable contributions to class discussions (he made an obscene joke about Henry VIII and everyone laughed). I look forward to watching his

progress in this subject (thank God he's not in my class next year).

GEOGRAPHY - 4D
Chloe is a pleasure to have in class (who the hell is she?). Quiet but studious (still can't place her) she gets on with her work with the minimum fuss. (Nope, completely eludes me. Will have to wing it on parents' evening.)

FRENCH - 3A
Washington is a true individual (the most pretentious name in class, which is going some given there are three Coopers, one Jaxon and a Boudicca) and his unique approach to his French (don't get me started) always challenges and stimulates (but not in a way that might exclude involvement with the police in the near future).

SPANISH - 3A
It is always interesting when Ethan puts his mind to Spanish – the results are fascinating and challenging (he speaks a version of Klingon, I think).

RELIGIOUS EDUCATION - 6A
Morgana's understanding of some of the less well-known religions always makes class discussions interesting (are you actually Druids yourselves?) and her practical demonstrations of knowledge in class are highly diverting (luckily we managed to avoid the other child's parents pressing charges).

ICT - 6A

James is a very gifted programmer (way beyond my skills – he left me behind in the second week) and has been very helpful to other students in the class (he's running the show; I'm just kicking back and thinking about Miss Bazakiel, the new French teacher). If he continues to work at this rate, he will do very well in next year's exam (and I won't have to teach the class for the rest of the year).

PSE (Personal and Social Education) - 7C

Having Joshua in the class when we were discussing bullying was very useful (he was curled up in the corner, sobbing). His contribution to the dramatic results of bullying had a powerful effect on the class (they all pointed at him and shouted 'loser'). I am sure that his confidence in the subject will improve over time (he sees the school psychiatrist next week).

PE - 5C

Samuel is a fun-loving student who clearly enjoys his sport (sitting on the sofa with a tub of ice cream). His enthusiasm is infectious (a pain in the class) and he has made good progress in his gym skills this term (he managed to get changed into his PE kit).

FORM TUTOR – This is an encouraging report, XX (insert student name here, I can't be arsed to do it now, I've got 30 more to do tonight) has made good progress, his/her learning targets are clear for next year. Enjoy the holiday. (I'm fucking off for six weeks now.)

❝ PARENTAL CHOICE ❞

'More wine? There you go. Where were we? Ah yes. Education. Well, I just don't see how you can be against PARENTAL CHOICE. My parents worked jolly hard to give me the sort of opportunity they were handed on a plate by their parents.

'They had to put me down for Weaton public school years before I was due to go. And I'm jolly glad they did.

'Of course, anyone can apply to have their son go to Weaton – it's not just there for the privileged and wealthy, you know. Fees are a very reasonable £10,000 – no, that's per term – but it's plain as a pikestaff that you really do get top facilities, smaller classes and an introduction to some first-rate coves. But you don't have to. I hear there are some quite reasonable grammar schools nowadays – academies, I think they call them. And all you have to do is buy a house close by – probably cheaper to pay the fees, all things considered. And then you're guaranteed to get little Boris into Oxbridge.

'But that's what's so marvellous about this country. Anyone can do it – that's why we call it PARENTAL CHOICE.'

❝ TRADITIONAL VALUES ❞

'In our school we believe that TRADITIONAL VALUES form the bedrock of a good education. Who hasn't found themselves in a tight corner and wished that they'd been able to draw on a list of the Kings and Queens of England? Who hasn't regretted not paying attention in trigonometry class whilst haggling with the timber department at B&Q? Well, fear not, should your little Johnny or Jenny be lucky enough to be admitted to our spanking new free school, we shall ensure that, if nothing else, they leave here intimate with both the Slide Rule and an in-depth knowledge of our glorious seafaring past.'

❝ ISN'T HER STRONGEST SUBJECT ❞

'It's Mr and Mrs Springer, isn't it? Yes, well, er, Jade? It is Jade, isn't it? Jade's had a challenging year. I think it would be fair to say that Maths ISN'T HER STRONGEST SUBJECT, although it might be fairer to say that we really have no idea, as she didn't really apply herself as we might have wished. When I say 'apply', I might as well say 'attend' because, frankly, I couldn't pick her out of a line-up of classmates even if she had the name 'Jade' pinned to her chest. I suppose I'm saying that there is more chance of Year 8 Maths solving Fermat's Last Theorem than of your little Jade turning up for three lessons in a row or, to put it another way, Maths really ISN'T HER STRONGEST SUBJECT.'

❝ UNIVERSITY ISN'T RIGHT FOR EVERYONE ❞

'UNIVERSITY ISN'T RIGHT FOR EVERYONE and some children will be much better served if they follow a vocational course, which has just as much merit in the eyes of employers as a university degree. So Tamara, for instance, never really got on at school, she's terrifically bright but in her own way. She adores horses, and they love her, so it seems much the best solution for her to work at the stables with a view to owning one very soon.'

❛ EXAMS ARE SO MUCH EASIER NOW THAN BEFORE ❜

'Nowadays children seem to be able to hand in so-called "course work", be "continually assessed" and tackle the dumbed-down curricula in a series of bite-sized modules, all of which has mainly been done, either by their parents, or cut and pasted from the Internet. Of course, "continual assessment" actually means "keep on taking the test until the teacher can't bear to look at the paper any more and gives you a good grade". Such exams as there are rely on guesswork (sorry, multiple choice) and pupils can take "study aids" (yes, "the answers") in with them. Back when I did school exams, an A meant an A. You felt that you had really achieved something after two years of intensive study. Challenging subjects (long-dead languages), informed teachers (using notes first compiled in a burst of enthusiasm 20 years ago), respectful students (beaten with anything wooden and nearby if they breathed loudly in class), knowledge that equipped you for life (I've never had to solve a differential equation since) and a rigorous three-hour exam at the end of the course (most of our generation are still getting over the psychological damage). Exams tested you then and were worth something.'

❮ SHE'S VERY CREATIVE ❯

'I don't know where she gets it from. I mean, yes, I went to stage school but I was never really that gifted, really, and as for Thomas, well, you know Thomas – not a creative bone in his body. Her last nanny was Brazilian and I think she picked up an extraordinary sense of rhythm from her.

'Her drama coach says she has great talent – can you believe? Her music teacher has been bandying the "P" word about, er, "Prodigy", but that's the last thing we want. I mean *the pressure*. She's already doing three languages (yes, including Latin), the violin, grade-five piano, ashtanga yoga – no, she's learning instruction – football, computer programming and horses – Mummy insisted *raises eyes to heavens* but what can you do? Would it be right not to let her flourish? SHE'S VERY CREATIVE. There are only so many hours in the day but we want her to get the best start and it is SO competitive out there these days. God knows what it's going to be like when she starts school. Oh, that's the alarm – she has taxidermy now. Must dash. Mwah mwah.'

❮ HE'S A TYPICAL TEENAGER! ❯

'Where did it all go wrong? I did all the right things when he was young now I can't make him do anything, even if I bribe him with loads of cash. (It's not that he'll turn out bad, it's just that I look so incompetent.)'

❝ SHE'S SO INDEPENDENT ❞

'Really, she totally looks after herself – gets herself ready and off to school in the morning. (She can't stand the sight of me at any time but mornings are particularly bad.) I often don't see her 'til after tea on school nights because she's off at a friend's house doing homework, or running the Junior Photography Club or playing netball (or round her boyfriend's house, or terrorising innocent pensioners at the local shopping centre). She has her own key of course and I sometimes get a quick catch-up but really her life is so busy I rarely get a look-in. (She's just getting used to leaving home as soon as she possibly can.)'

❝ WE MAKE SURE THAT WE HAVE FAMILY TIME EVERY DAY ❞

'The kids are such free spirits and have so many interests; and of course they're typical teenagers so they spend as much time as they can looking at screens of all shapes and sizes. That's why WE MAKE SURE THAT WE HAVE FAMILY TIME EVERY DAY. It doesn't have to be long, but we feel it's really important just to have that face-to-face time to catch up and find out what's been going on. (We're far too busy at work and have no energy when we get back to do anything other than grunt at each other as we pass in the kitchen. We're in competition to see who can spend the least time with the little bastards. To be frank, they could be dealing drugs from the house and we'd never know.)'

WHAT CHILDREN MEAN WHEN THEY SAY...

'But I want it...'
(Terrible twos tantrum on the way...)

'It's not fair...'
(See above.)

'I don't like it'
(It's not chocolate.)

'Bieber isn't sharing'
(I want to play with that toy now. On my own.
And I won't share it either.)

❝ NOW, LET'S NOT DO THAT, SHALL WE? ❞

A phrase that parents of the '40s and '50s would have balked at. Their equivalent was a whack across the top of the head and a 'No tea for you', as you were marched to your room. Today, and this is symptomatic of the parenting change we noted above, parents want to negotiate rather than beat, so now the children do the beating. It all works out in the end.

❛ THE TERRIBLE TWOS ❜

THE TERRIBLE TWOS is used to excuse any display of rage by a child between the ages of 18 months and 3-and-a-half years. The rage can occur anywhere – the supermarket, Granny's house, the police station – and is usually of such ferocity that it would make Attila the Hun look like a Liberal Democrat. Parents, at a total loss as to what to do, utter the words with a grimace, as if trying to explain the behaviour with a 'What-can-you-do?' linguistic shrug.

❛ WE'LL SEE ❜

The stock response to the most outrageous ('He's so ambitious – quite the little Duncan Bannatyne') request from a child. 'WE'LL SEE' trades on the cherished one's short attention span (the adult hopes) to deflect attention from his temporary (but repeated) infatuation with Lego Star Wars Millennium Falcon/Sony PSP/iPad (delete as appropriate) or more workaday demands such as a third ice cream, another hot chocolate or the desire to have a sociopathic friend round for a sleepover. 'WE'LL SEE' works up to a point when the child uses it against you: 'Could you tidy your room, please?' 'WE'LL SEE'.

MODERN BRITISH BABY NAMES

Chastiti – she whose name will soon be considered ironic

Maddison – bonkers

Olivia – she whose parents liked *The Waltons*

Harry – literally 'Home ruler'; figuratively middle-class scamp

Sophie – destined to work in PR or publishing

Charles – unlikely to cause trouble; high-income

Addison – conceived in a taxi

Jayden – he whose education is to be fitful

Camilla – acerbic; good teeth

Kyle – analytical, direct, forthright, uncoverer of secrets; illegitimate

❝ I'M BORED ❞

People get bored all over the world. They do. So what's so very British about being bored? Well, it's a combination of factors but particularly our ghastly 'temperate' climate and our high population density, which means, for many children, the double whammy of not being able to play in the rainy garden, should one be available, or safely on the streets. Of course, being confined 'inside' isn't so much of a penance for the average child now, who, surveys show, spend 96.7 per cent of their time posting soon-to-be-regretted photos and status updates on social media sites, or at worst killing a miscellany of characters on whatever video game happens to be in vogue. In the olden days of the 1960s, '70s and '80s though, it was tough – plastic toys or, worse, books were the only refuge from the creeping mind-paralysis brought on by semi-permanent incarceration in the home. This is why school holidays stretched, and why Steve McQueen's bouts of solitary confinement in the endlessly repeated, ironically titled *The Great Escape* resonated so strongly for millions of kids (and their parents). And why so many recited the mantra 'I'M BORED' in between bouts of torturing their siblings.

'BECAUSE I SAY SO' is the British parent's weapon of last resort. After bribes have been scorned, cajoling has fallen on deaf ears, threats have been derided, emotional blackmail hasn't softened the child's steadfast resolve and begging has been pitilessly ignored, there's only this nuclear option left in the armoury. Faced with the adorable offspring's defiance and implacable logic, the only way forward is to ignore reason and bully them into submission –'BECAUSE I SAY SO' is the verbal equivalent of twisting a child's arm behind his back and frog-marching him off to jail (or school as it's also known).

BIRTHS, MARRIAGES, DEATHS & RELATIONSHIPS

'**It was the best of times,** it was the worst of times' might equally apply to those celebrations we've grouped here as births, deaths, marriages and Christmas (we've also chucked in a confetti of observations on relationships, just to fill in the gaps).

It is events like these that make you wonder how Britain would cope without alcohol – not only does it oil the wheels of celebration or commemoration, but it allows many of those present to function in a basic fashion for a while, often before going completely off the rails.

If you doubt the truth of this, ask yourself this simple question: how many other countries commonly have fights at weddings?

There are many expressions and phrases perfunctorily rolled out on these occasions, to paper over the gaping emotional wounds being inflicted on the participants, or to avoid the need to think before speaking.

BIRTHS

When friends or family bring a new being into the world, both your relationship with them and the language you use changes. Gone are the carefree nights unencumbered by dashing home for the babysitter; gone too are the roaming discussions of everything and nothing; instead there are whole tracts of conversational landscape peppered with 'Here be landmines' signs. In this danger zone you have to tread incredibly carefully: the mines are set to explode at anything less than 100 per cent adoration of baby or 100 per cent admiration of parenting skills. We Brits are not always great at this, and tend to fall back on a few well-worn phrases, delivered with all the panache of an am-dram technical rehearsal.

❛ WHAT A BEAUTIFUL BABY! ❜

'WHAT A BEAUTIFUL BABY! (Ugh, what is that thing suffocating in a sick blanket?) Gosh isn't she (taking a bit of a gamble here, could be a boy) gorgeous? I'm not sure who she takes after most (God help her if she turns out like either of you to be honest). Congratulations! (Enjoy the next five years of not going out at all.) See you soon. (Looking even more careworn and bedraggled than you do now.)'

❝ HE HAS HIS FATHER'S / MOTHER'S / EYES / MOUTH / COLOURING / HAIR / SMILE ❞

This is the phrase of last resort: confronted with a face that defies any kind of compliment, pick a possible progenitor and the first feature that springs to mind and combine in a single sentence accompanied by a winning smile. The result will be a ten-minute discussion about the likeness of other features to other family members, which should make any further compliments unnecessary. A classic British compromise.

RELATIONSHIPS

What is a British relationship and how does it express itself differently from relationships in other parts of the world? Well, the obvious qualities that set at least some of us apart are extreme self-consciousness and self-deprecation, an inability to be direct and our ironic sense of everything, or at least this is what the Americans tell us (brash, vulgar dullards – we're being ironic, of course). Where better (*David Attenborough voice*) to view these qualities than in the personal ad – those former smudgy, desperate boxes at the back of the newspaper, crammed full of phrases like 'Tall non-smoker WLTM short non-smoker – GSOH BDSM GCH preferred', because we had to pay for them by the word. Now they are fully fledged multimedia events with photos (usually WAY out of date or of someone else entirely), and video messages directed by Hollywood A-listers.

MAN SEEKING WOMAN

What's the worst that can happen?[1] I've been on this site for ten months and met some amazing people[2] but not The One[3].

A few things about me which might help you to change your life[4] – I'm no spring chicken[5] but my friends say I'm good-looking[6]. I love to cook[7], spend the evening out with friends[8], go to the cinema for something arty[9] or the latest blockbuster. My job is quite stressful[10] so at the weekends I like to relax[11] – maybe a long country walk followed by a great pub lunch[12]? I play quite a lot of sports for my age[13] – badminton, tennis, football, marathon running, fencing, and cricket – and I like to keep in shape.

What am I looking for in a partner?[14] Well, you'll be easy-going[15], like socialising and have a good sense of humour[16]. Looks aren't important[17] – you can't tell much from a photo[18], it's all about the chemistry[19], and we'll know as soon as we meet. Don't delay – this offer won't last long![20]

1. Assault? Murder? Rabbit roasting?
2. Easy lays
3. See above but with money
4. Get a restraining order
5. More like a frozen turkey
6. The friends in my head
7. I own a microwave
8. Get pissed in pubs
9. *Knocked Up* – that's arty
10. For my colleagues mainly
11. Drink to oblivion
12. See above
13. Just letting you know I'm in Great Physical Shape
14. Sex mainly – definitely not commitment unless you're loaded
15. Possibly via medication
16. You'll need one
17. I'm desperate
18. Certainly not mine, it's one of Hugh Grant I cut out of *The Sun*
19. Alcohol
20. My six-month subscription runs out next week

WOMAN SEEKING MAN

I'm a happy, bubbly person[1], who doesn't take life too seriously[2]. I love living in the city[3] and I love all it has to offer[4].

A random list of things I love would include: dogs and cats[5]; tea and cake[6]; laughter and tears[7]; wine and fires[8]; walking and talking; cuddling and watching a great film[9]. I like putting the world to rights over a bottle of wine[10] and as long as you share my broadly leftish world view[11] we should get along fine. I also like exclamation marks!!!!![12].

If you are house-trained and have your own teeth that'd be a good start[13]. Seriously, though I'm looking for someone I can share the fun times with: looking up at the sky through the trees[14], loving urban chaos[15]; peering at old books[16]; and escaping for a weekend of passion in the country[17] — as well as someone who will be there for me when the going gets tough[18]. Solvent and professional a must[19]. Getting on with kids would also be an advantage[20] as would a great sense of humour[21]. Well, what are you waiting for?[22]

1. Uh-oh
2. UHH-OHH
3. I don't really have a choice because of the kids
4. Over-priced restaurants you can't get into; crammed, miserable tube trains; paranoid strangers
5. Well cats, but I don't want to put you off
6. A bit too much
7. Mainly tears, these days
8. A lethal combination, but there you go
9. You may have read some of this somewhere else
10. OK – three
11. Pretending to empathise with people who frankly scare me
12. That's me being funny
13. But it's by no means a deal breaker

14. Kooky? Moi?
15. Well, I prefer Dorothy Perkins,
but that's for me to know
16. Well, my London *A–Z* is from 1998
17. Premier Inn, Hammersmith,
will do at a push

18. QUITE a lot actually
19. I don't do quirky and penniless
any more – ideally looking to pool
houses within three months
20. Since I have six of them
21. See above
22. Hello? Hello…?

'I REALLY LIKE YOU, (Beware: there's a huge three-letter word on its way...) BUT (there it is) I'm not sure that we're ultimately meant to be together (in fact I'm bloody positive we're not). I know we've had a lovely time and it all seems great but I can't help wanting a bit, you know, more (I'm sooo bored hearing about your job/mum/car/life and I'm actually much better suited to the really fit bloke I met at the gym last week). It really isn't you, it's all down to me (it's definitely you) and I'm really, really sorry (can I go now, please?). We can stay in touch, if you want to, and there'll always be an affectionate place in my heart for you (Christ, am I really saying this? I can feel a stomach tsunami on the rise). I know, I'm so sorry. OK. Are you sure you'll be OK? (Here's the number for Samaritans.) OK. Just call me any time you want to talk (must order that new SIM card). Bye. You're sure you'll be OK? OK. Take care. Bye. Bye.'

WEDDINGS

Weddings are where you come face-to-face with those relatives the memory of whose existence you had forcibly suppressed deep over the course of many years. There are a number of useful stock phrases you can employ while you try frantically to remember who you're talking to and whether they've got any awkward family circumstances you should avoid mentioning:

'Gosh, it's cousin Emily isn't it? It's been years. How are you? And those lovely kids of yours? Still a bit of a handful? Therapy, you say? Sorry not to have been in touch but we do so enjoy reading your Christmas letters – too funny. Yes, we're fine. Soldiering on – you know, can't wait for the fledglings to spread their wings and fly but slightly dreading the quiet as well. Well, so lovely to see you. Which table are you on? Nine? Ah, great, same as us. So we'll... um, see you later!'

'WE'VE BEEN SO LUCKY WITH THE WEATHER'

(It's been raining on and off for the past six months and I nearly had to wear white wellies under the dress.)

'WOULD YOU LIKE SOME SPARKLING WINE?'

(It was going to be champagne but the bride's father got jettisoned by RBS last month and is currently 'finding himself' up a hill in Mongolia with a shaman.)

DEATHS

Funerals are never easy affairs. We British are expert at making them even more uncomfortable than elsewhere in the world by our rigid non-displays of emotion. While we seem perfectly happy (and indeed very good at) collective grief-gushes when it comes to minor celebs and members of the Royal Family, when it comes to our nearest and dearest we have complete emotion-fail. We stand around redefining the word 'awkward' with every uncomfortable word and gesture. Here are some of the phrases that we use:

❝ IT'S WHAT HE WOULD HAVE WANTED ❞

'A nice service attended by his family – not that they got on, but IT'S WHAT HE WOULD HAVE WANTED. In fact he couldn't even stand to be in the same room as his cousin Jack but IT'S WHAT HE WOULD HAVE WANTED, in the end.

'We couldn't decide whether to go for the expensive casket or the biodegradable one so we opted for the cheaper – we're sure IT'S WHAT HE WOULD HAVE WANTED.

'Afterwards we're going back to Jack's for a few drinks to celebrate the miserable old goat's life – it'll be the only time he's been sociable for 30 years and he's dead, but IT'S WHAT HE WOULD HAVE WANTED.'

❝ SHE HAD A GOOD INNINGS ❞

> *'Amazing really when you think she was 97. So full of life and always a character. Never tired of her practical jokes, did she? Remember the one with the glass of sherry and the hard-boiled egg. Legend. We'll miss her but SHE HAD A GOOD INNINGS. Of course when her memory started to go and she thought she was working in the munitions factory again during the war, that was a bit of a worry – particularly when she started experimenting with the bleach and nail-polish remover in the kitchen. Never could explain that one properly to the fire brigade. Still she survived and SHE HAD A GOOD INNINGS.'*

CHRISTMAS

And finally, a brief glossary for the ultimate family occasion: Christmas. If there was a prize for the most bilious and stressful annual holiday, the season of goodwill would win hands down every year. The tension is apparent even as the presents are being unwrapped...

'You can take it back, I kept the receipts just in case'
(I grabbed the nearest thing I could find – frankly I thought it was hideous but couldn't be bothered to spend a second longer on you...)

'Thank you – it's just what I wanted'
(Ten years ago, Granny.)

'Would anyone like champagne?'
(It's a race to see who can become unconscious first and avoid trying to construct Camilla's fairy castle.)

'What's on telly?'
(I'd rather watch a boxed set of *Cash in the Attic* than listen to the rest of you for another minute.)

'It's the worst Christmas ever'
('Until the next one.')

'He's just a bit over-excited'
(Has anyone got any tranquilisers? Montgomery's on a toddler bender and we'll be heading to A&E very shortly.)

The British attitude to tucker is complicated and class ridden, this is reflected in the way we talk about and describe our food. Until the 1960s it was pretty straightforward – you ate as well as you could afford to and the times allowed. Post-war rationing had an enormous effect on the British psyche – people ate whatever they could acquire for their families – scarcity meant taste became secondary to volume.

With the increasing affluence of British society in the '60s and '70s came 'taste without taste' – we demanded more from the food on our plate but, lacking an ingrained food culture similar to the French, Italians or South Americans, we were in a poor position to judge whether we were getting the real thing. A culture of suspicion evolved – eating at a fancy French restaurant was a mark of sophistication but we lacked the tools to judge whether what we were served was actually any good or not.

Then the big food giants stepped in to tell us what we liked – what was good and what wasn't – and we generally breathed a sigh of relief. Like children, we relinquished control and gratefully accepted the stodgy pizzas, molten curries and MSG-filled pot-noodle food which today is the fat-congested heart of the British diet.

This complicated history and our consequent general distrust of food is well reflected in the language we use to talk about it, describe it or, mainly, justify it.

HOME-PREPARED

'All our food is HOME-PREPARED on the premises. The weekly delivery of frozen meals from an articulated lorry is sorted by hand and stored in the kitchen freezer. As our staff take your individual lunch and dinner orders, chef selects each portion by hand and, taking care to remove all the wrappings, lovingly heats them through in the microwave oven until each component of your HOME-PREPARED meal is piping hot. If he is simultaneously heating two or more portions, he takes care to ensure all the ingredients have been heated through, often checking once more by hand. Your HOME-PREPARED food is then freshly brought (by hand) to your table for your eating enjoyment.'

❝ I THINK I'LL HAVE THE... ❞

'Tasting menu'
(Smaller portions for more money. The FOOD WANKER'S fantasy dinner.)

Small plates
(See tasting menu.)

'Modern British'
(Anything which sounds like an appalling fusion of medieval peasant food and weeds, e.g. 'Lamb sweetbreads with dandelion fricassée and a ragwort *jus*.')

'Chef's special'
(What we couldn't sell last week, or got a special deal on from the suppliers. On the plus side it might not have to be defrosted.)

'Value ready meal'
(Contains at least 39 per cent horse.)

❪ GOING FOR A CURRY ❫

GOING FOR A CURRY in Britain is akin to having a cup of tea in Japan – it could be a simple affair or a full-blown ceremony with rigid rules to be observed before the curry can be considered properly 'gone for'. Alcohol is, of course, central, as it is to most aspects of British culture.

At the easy end of Balti Street lies the ubiquitous supermarket, with its bland, boot-polish-red chicken tikka masala, poppadoms and pilau rice for home consumption, after a five-minute zapping with microwaves. At the far end of Balti Street sits the local Taj Mahal or Kashmir restaurant with its bland, boot-polish-red chicken tikka masala, poppadoms and pilau rice for sit-in consumption after a five-minute zapping with microwaves.

So what's the difference between these two experiences? Well, traditionally the Taj Mahal was only approached at 10.55pm on a Friday or Saturday night after a ritual ten pints of lager, whisky chaser and two packets of crisps – consumed at a pub within staggering distance of the curry house. The diners would enter the premises in an advanced state of inebriation, loudly and cheerily insult the staff with some casual, off-the-cuff racist banter, annoy any other customers fool enough to be present at these ceremonial times, and then order more lager and salty poppadoms to keep the party going. They would then spend several minutes studying the menu before going for one of two options – the aforementioned chicken tikka/pilau combo, or the notorious, spicy vindaloo. Probably the worst thing to eat, gastrically speaking, after consuming a gallon of cold, fizzy lager, chicken, lamb or beef vindaloo was for decades the 'go-to' curry for the non-discerning, inebriated curry fiend. In many ways, the 'V Loo' was the night-cap to end all night-caps, and a sharp reminder of what you had been up to the night before, should the memories be a little blurry. Ladies, should any be unwisely present, might sensibly go for a mild 'korma' but the bleary-eyed alpha male of the party would see it as his duty to accept the ring-of-fire challenge proffered by the battered, stained cardboard menu.

Nowadays the Indian restaurant experience, like all dining experiences, has been given an upgrade, and all manner of regional authentic and boutique dishes are now zapped in the microwave for five minutes before being served with poppadoms and, oh, maybe a glass of lukewarm white wine. Has something been lost from the experience? Probably not, but there has definitely been a change in GOING FOR A CURRY.

❝ WOULD YOU LIKE TO SEE THE WINE LIST? ❞

The Money Pit. How restaurants pay the bills. 'Here's five pounds' worth of booze – now give me 25 quid.' To most UK citizens, the wine list begins and ends at page one – 'house – red or white'. Venturing beyond that into the world of fine wine is akin to stepping beyond these shores armed with only the most rudimentary tools of language – we tend to be guided by price ('£26 should do it') and view the promises of 'Blackcurrant and tobacco aromas', 'A foxy, farmyard intensity' or a 'Long, chewy finish' with the same distrust we regard a German in possession of a rolled-up beach towel.

'WE USE NOTHING BUT **FRESH** INGREDIENTS'

(Ingredients which have almost certainly been frozen at least once, but are not made of metal or plastic.)

'WOULD YOU LIKE SOME JUS?'

('Would you like a dribble of pretentious gravy?')

'FREE FROM ARTIFICIAL COLOURS OR PRESERVATIVES'

(Contains enough salt to de-ice the M4 and enough sugar to caramelise it.)

RESTAURANT CRITICS

British RESTAURANT CRITICS are loathed and loved in equal measure – mainly by themselves. The daring chroniclers of British Food Culture, the Wise Men guided by one or two stars to newly opened premises right across London. They rarely venture further afield unless on a joyless weekend break – oh, they'll make sure it sounds joyless – because that would be too much like hard work and besides, what can possibly happen outside London that would be worth writing about? Funny how they all end up reviewing the same places – you would think they were immune to PR.

Quite often the offspring of talented journalists and broadcasters, they have achieved their status purely on merit, and therefore feel no compunction about destroying the livelihood of someone who has trained and worked their fingers to the bone for years with a single withering sentence, maybe because the chef had an off day or the critic's car was broken into that morning. Theirs is an essentially trivial occupation yet they must take their weekly assessments of the state of London gastronomy seriously enough to persuade the magazines and newspapers that it's worth coughing up a few grand every week to regurgitate 'The liquorice-smoked chicken skin is the best in Hoxton' all over the country. Maybe it's this cognitive dissonance that induces the hunger necessary to eat for free in so many restaurants, week after week, month after month, year after year, without shame or being able to maintain a sense of perspective.

They've mastered the necessary self-deprecation but occasionally lapse into self-importance – only once every three or four sentences, say – just to let you know that they are authorities, on top of all things gastro and gastric, and really should be taken seriously. Because if you don't take them seriously, who on earth is going to?

CHEF'S TABLE

Most chefs are bonkers, egotistical and bad-tempered. Well, the good ones, anyway. Why on earth would you pay extra to sit close to them, especially if you're British? The reason we have separate rooms in restaurants for preparing and serving food is exactly so you never have to set eyes on an overweight, foul-mouthed nutter ripping the cheeks off a pig. This is an act of pure masochism – like sitting at the front of class in the hope of scoring Brownie points, while everyone flicks blotting paper at your back. In France it's possible that the diners and staff might enjoy a convivial evening discussing the *terroir* of the wine or the provenance of the wild mushrooms. Here it's more likely that a hapless client will end up in casualty with a cleaver in his back or an arm frozen in liquid nitrogen.

VEGETARIAN

A phrase that used to mean 'Without…'. As in, 'Rump steak, chips and vegetables, without the steak'; 'Seared pork loin, mashed potato, vegetables and jus without the pork loin'. At a push, somewhere posh (i.e. with two microwave ovens) you might be offered 'vegetable moussaka' – a deadly nuclear fission pie of a dish – or mushrooms with, well, mainly mushrooms, truth be told. Now most reasonable restaurants make an effort to include at least one bona fide VEGETARIAN dish on the menu – goats' cheese tart, usually – which is only there for window dressing because the assumption kind of persists that, if you're a VEGETARIAN, you really don't like food that much and have no place being in a restaurant at all. Not quite as bad as a paedophile on the school staff, but in the same ballpark.

DEEP-FRIED

Now you're talking! DEEP-FRIED could happily replace the 'Great' in Great Britain as far as the majority of our obesity-prone populace is concerned. People who don't like deep-fried food in Britain are viewed with great suspicion – what kind of person wouldn't want to take a tasty fillet of fish and batter the hell out of it until all you can taste is a crisp, oily sludge? Probably a VEGETARIAN. As for chips, even fanatical foodies look a little crestfallen when they're presented with a menu not offering the 'side' option of fries – cooked in a reassuringly pretentious method, of course: 'The veal dripping is extraordinary and the fat absorption cuts through the sweet calf juices.'

POP-UP RESTAURANT

The FOOD WANKER'S fantasy location. Proof that if you queue for long enough you'll find anything you're served subsequently delicious and innovative, maybe even 'challenging'.

FOOD WANKERS

Urban sophisticates who measure their self-worth by their foodie degrees of separation from the rest of us. These people swing in the opposite direction, embracing any trend as fulsomely as the average Brit views it with suspicion. The FOOD WANKERS championed nouvelle cuisine in the '80s, 'authentic' food in the '90s, and these days pretty much anything they are told is different by a handful of media food commentators. These are the poor souls who stand for three hours in the pouring rain to be fed a deconstructed hamburger with quadruple-cooked chips at a POP-UP RESTAURANT in East London, simply so they can convince themselves that they are part of a vibrant food culture and that Britain is leading the way in bold and interesting cuisine. Still, it keeps them happy and keeps the restaurant tills ker-chinging away merrily.

SHOPPING &
COMPLAINING

Shopping and complaining are two of our favourite pastimes, even though we're crap at both of them. Napoleon is alleged to have used the phrase 'A nation of shopkeepers' (originally coined by Adam Smith in 1776) to describe the British. Well, times have changed and latterly we have become more like a nation of empty retail outlets and offshore tax-avoidance merchants. Where once the 'vibrant' (see under 'rose-tinted spectacles') High Street was the only place to shop, now we can click away and never have to negotiate a customer experience with a bored, hostile teenager. We are, however, inveterate shoppers and the streak of masochism runs deep in the national psyche. So the litter-strewn High Street of the 1970s and '80s has been replaced by American-style malls and out-of-town 'retail parks' but the language of shopping – the words we use in the rare interactions – have remained pretty much the same. In truth, there's no better place in Britain to spot the English language (and British character) in action than when on a visit 'to the shops'.

While at the shops, 'If you don't mind me saying', 'Sorry about this', and 'I couldn't help noticing' are all classic British opening gambits for a game of Complaint. Although we may have improved our technique slightly, after decades of American culture have slightly permeated our determinedly subservient attitude to any service or product provider, the British are still world-class bad at registering notice of dissatisfaction.

In Britain the phrase 'CAN I HELP YOU?' uttered by a menacing teenage shop assistant can be the most threatening expression in the English language. It could even partly explain why we have taken up online shopping with such unfettered enthusiasm. Unlike in other countries where shop assistants seem genuinely to want to 'help', here the words mean the exact opposite. It is a phrase of such hostile intent that to take up the offer the shopper risks the ultimate in retail disaster: humiliation in front of fellow customers.

❛ CAN I ORDER IT FOR YOU? ❜

Something in the forlorn eyes of the shop assistant tells you that he knows you're just going to check the barcode on the product with your smartphone and order it from Amazon (other online retailers are available – for the moment anyway) the moment he speaks these words. There is tragedy in the words too – the words contain the very reason for the boarded-up, empty lots on the High Street and point to the imminent 'repurposing' of the assistant's own career as the shop heads towards the retail graveyard.

SUPERMARKETS

SUPERMARKETS are emblematic of many changes that have occurred in Britain in the past decades. Newsagents, butchers, grocers, clothes shops and even travel agents have all been vacuumed up from our High Streets and spat into monster emporiums and vast hypermarket spaces on the edge of towns. These huge corporations control almost every aspect of retail left unhoovered by the offshore, online pirates and bring convenience, low prices and ample parking as their pay-off for fucking up our neighbourhoods. And lots of part-time, insecure, underpaid bang-your-own-head-on-a-spike-for-job-satisfaction employment opportunities for the people who otherwise would have worked in the grocers, butchers, clothes shops and travel agents that have disappeared.

'Unexpected item in bagging area – please wait for assistance'

(We think you are trying to steal from us, but it would be bad if we screamed, 'Stop there arsehole! You're surrounded by minimum-wage students, pensioners and mums – do you really think you'll make it out alive?' every time one of you misplaces a box of cornflakes.)

'Colleague alert – spillage in aisle 27'

(How much do you need this job, Davies? You may have been in middle-management for the past 20 years but you're ours now. Run, you fat fucker!)

'Buy one, get one free'

(You don't even want ONE really, do you?)

❛ CAN I GIFT-WRAP THAT FOR YOU? ❜

This is a relatively recent re-introduction to the British High Street. The days are long gone when purchases were wrapped up in unbranded paper and tied in string. Nowadays everything must be branded to increase the retailer's profile – plastic bags are still the weapon of choice – but recently gift-wrapping has entered the fray. It's good for those customers (OK, men) who loathe wrapping presents but can provoke much tutting and sighing from anyone behind them in the queue who just want to pay and clear off.

❛ SOURCED FROM PRODUCERS WHO SHARE OUR VALUES ❜

It must have been a very harmonious meeting: farmer, supermarket executive and chicken representatives all sitting down to discuss their values and, hallelujah, it turned out that they already had matching views on just about everything: the war in Afghanistan, population growth, gun control in America and battery farming. Wasn't that lucky?

RETAIL THERAPY

When we Brits muster the courage to talk frankly about the disappointing levels of 'service' we have been subjected to, our complaints are, for the comfort of everyone, handled as non-confrontationally as possible. Whenever possible we are encouraged to make our opinions known on the phone or by email. In such situations, it has become part of good 'customer relations' to trot out some of these stock phrases:

❝ WE ARE COMMITTED TO IMPROVING THE CUSTOMER EXPERIENCE ❞

There was a time when the word 'experience' used to signify something and 'having an experience' meant doing something significant. Now we use the word to indicate that we have inhaled and exhaled somewhere.

❛ IS THERE ANYTHING ELSE I CAN HELP YOU WITH TODAY? ❜

No matter how much grief you offload on the unfortunate customer liaison executive, or how little your 25 minutes on hold and two minutes of shouting has achieved, the script demands that every conversation should end on a smiley note of 'Here to help'. Hence this killer line at the end of your unresolved complaint. Whether it is calculated to raise your blood pressure still further or is a means of IMPROVING THE CUSTOMER EXPERIENCE to that of near-hospitalisation is moot, but it invariably ensures that the phone becomes yet another victim of domestic violence.

QUEUEING

The Queue Eye – watching for a surreptitious self-insertion – is another one of those traits that highlights the best and worst of British behaviour. We believe in the fairness of the queue – that it is a leveller which transcends one's place in the social order – so we don't like it when we hear of people being paid to queue on behalf of someone else to save them 23 dreary, drizzly hours of exposure to claim the new iTablet or outer-court Wimbledon tickets. It challenges the supposedly innate British SENSE OF FAIR PLAY (see p.14). On the other hand we are sometimes maybe a little too uptight about the observance of the queuing procedure – to the point where we get upset, maybe even a little feisty, when a late arrival joins a friend in the queue in front of us, having the temerity to do so without giving handwritten apologies to every person who has been relegated a single space by this inconsiderate behaviour. Such action is likely to be greeting with an outbreak of 'tutting' and scowls but, of course, with us being British, no actual complaints.

Here are some other phrases you might hear in a British queue:

'DO YOU MIND IF I GO AHEAD OF YOU? I ONLY HAVE A BOTTLE OF MILK'

('My time is so much more important than yours.')

'DO YOU WANT ANY HELP WITH YOUR PACKING?'

('Would you like your bread squashed by some cans of dog food, and your fruit pulped by tinned vegetables?')

CALL CENTRES

The one thing that does seem to stir our blood and brings out our inner bulldog is having to complain to some poor sod in a CALL CENTRE. The extent of our reaction depends, partly at least, on location, location, location…

Call centre in Liverpool

Call centre in Ireland

Call centre in US

Call centre in Egypt

Call centre in India

This is inexplicable. There is no earthly reason why a knowledgeable young person in Delhi should be considered less helpful in dealing with our queries than one in Liverpool, but we are determined that it be so. Maybe it's a hangover from the good old colonial days – we don't like being told what to do by people who we used to tell what to do. Maybe there's a subconscious fear that being connected to Somewhere Far Away must be costing a fortune and someone's going to have to pay. Whatever reasons lie behind it, the Indian Call Centre has passed into British folklore as a symbol of dishonest corporate behaviour – and has itself become something to complain about.

❝ I DON'T MEAN TO COMPLAIN BUT... ❞

So bad are we at complaining, so mortifying do we find the prospect of conflict, no matter how impersonal the dispute may be, that our complaints frequently end up becoming apologies. Apologies, that is, for the inadequacy of the service or product that has been provided to us, in return for our hard-earned money, by the other party. It's our fault for not anticipating, we instinctively feel. For going with the cheapest quote, for choosing that brand of washing machine unaware of its propensity to leak 20 gallons of water into our downstairs neighbour's kitchen ('Sorry about that, too'). The frequently quoted equation 'Tragedy plus time equals comedy' can be adapted to explain the British attitude to complaining: 'Complaint plus time equals apology'.

We do have a tendency to cave in when faced with a bit of resistance. No wonder Americans (and the French, Australians, Germans, Albanians etc.) think we're losers…

'I'm sorry, I think the scallops may have given my wife food poisoning – she died this morning – of course it might not have been the scallops. Has anyone else died who ate here yesterday, do you know? Don't worry, I can phone back later, if that's all right?'

'We couldn't help noticing the car seemed to have developed a small problem – probably nothing to worry about really – when the engine burst into flames and the seat covers melted. We just wondered, as we bought the car last week, if that would possibly be covered by the warranty? No? Oh, OK then.'

'Sorry, if you don't mind me asking – is that how the roof is going to look? Because we quite liked it all the same colour. Oh, how much more expensive? I see. Was that in your quote? Oh, it's my fault, I should have asked for a breakdown, yes. Never mind, I'll, er, go and make us all a cup of tea…'

'I don't like to complain but we did book to go to Madeira and, unless I'm very much mistaken, this is Estonia. Yes, they do sound a bit similar, don't they? Yes, true, this is a hotel. Yes, minus-20 degrees and plus-20 aren't really all that different I suppose when you put it like that. You see, I don't really have any warm clothes with me – just T-shirts and shorts. Where? The Kristiine Shopping Centre? The 2, 3, 6 trolley buses? Er, thank you…'

'I don't want to be any trouble but I was only in here to have a mole removed – isn't that my nose? Do you think I might have it back? Not that I want to be any trouble.'

❝ YOUR CALL IS IMPORTANT TO US ❞

'...please don't hang up because YOUR CALL IS IMPORTANT TO US – so important that we've installed this automated answering service which prevents you from speaking to a live human being, unless you can select the right combination of 81 in-call options, which will take you through to our customer service centre in Calcutta – if you're lucky – or the one just outside Glasgow if you guess incorrectly. You will subsequently be quizzed by a disinterested, otherwise unemployable customer services representative, reading from a script on their PC screen so, to be honest, you might as well accept that, one way or another, YOUR CALL, WHICH IS VERY IMPORTANT TO US, will be dealt with by a computer in an almost certainly unsatisfactory manner. If you would like to hear some urban music now, press 1, to listen to pop, press 2, if classical is more your thing, press 3. To induce a brain haemorrhage press the hash key at any time. Thank you for holding...'

TROLLING

It's a different matter when we Brits can make our complaint anonymously – like in the 'comments' section that follow many online newspaper articles, for example. Here we see the dark underbelly of the Internet: green ink flowing through the computer keyboard of 'trolls' – generally sad, angry little individuals looking to provoke a response rather than contribute to the debate. Trolls exist worldwide, of course, but there is something about the British temperament – our legendary repression of emotions and feelings perhaps – which lends itself to vicious no-holds-barred vitriol-pouring when no one knows our identity. We become the granny at the wrestling, all inhibitions thrown off, pummelling someone three times her size with a handbag full of chocolate limes...

❛ JUST BROWSING ❜

The best (and probably only) defence against 'CAN I HELP YOU?' is 'JUST BROWSING', a phrase that is as dismissive as 'CAN I HELP YOU?' is aggressive. It sends the signal that the shopper doesn't want to engage with the shop assistant on any level – a kind of negotiated truce. Of course, this is the perfect state of affairs for our non-confrontational natures and can lead to a completely harmonious non-interaction – the perfect shopping experience.

And finally, the word that defines us; the word that seems to start most sentences and hovers over every occasion like a pigeon waiting to drop its breakfast; the word that should be the first to be attempted by a British baby and the word that, to adapt Elton John, seems to be the commonest word: 'SORRY'. It can be used regardless of the situation – there is almost no occasion where some form of apology is inappropriate – and can almost always be relied upon to fill the awkward silences which all British people fear.

For most British people 'SORRY' is rarely a simple word of apology for a transgression committed by the speaker. Rather it is the tacit acknowledgement that something irregular has occurred between two or more people which requires a speedy response lest it should escalate in significance and require a more fulsome reaction. Hence the chain of sorries often induced by the initial ejaculation – it's like dampening a fire before it bursts out of control, and this frequently requires the offended party to join in with the sorries. It also explains why, in so many cases, 'SORRY' is followed by 'but' – to contradict or point out an error (regardless of the perpetrator) requires an apology above all else.

Here are some common deployments of the word, as well as some exceptional occurrences.

SORRY STATE OF AFFAIRS

'We're sorry you're leaving us'
(…although we were wondering how much longer we'd have to put up with your egg sandwiches, hyena cackle, dubious hygiene, endless sick days, smoker's cough, eggy farts and passive-aggressive ways. Good luck in your new job.)

'Sorry, can I just get past?'
'Sorry, can I just squeeze past to get some yoghurt? (You've been standing here for two minutes looking at the double cream and I really need to get on.) So, can I just get by? (I really don't want to touch you because I haven't ruled out the possibility that you have the Ebola virus, but I don't want to appear rude.)'

'Sorry, can I just stop you there?'
(You've been wanging on about your own particular bugbear for three minutes, which is two minutes 50 seconds longer than I was actually interested.)

❝ SORRY, BUT I THINK YOU'RE WRONG ❞

In any other language, a straightforward 'No, I completely disagree' would not be preceded by a 'SORRY'; but in English, it is the correct formulation. Disagreements, unless fuelled by strong lager, are generally to be avoided but if you do feel that your opponent has overstepped a mark, be sure to preface your counter-argument with the 'S' word. This is the most confrontational use of 'SORRY' to be heard in the British Isles – the verbal equivalent of the pit bull terrier.

❝ WE'RE SORRY YOU'RE DISAPPOINTED WITH OUR SERVICE ❞

'We're sorry you found our customer service's response to your complaint disappointing. At [insert multinational name here] we pride ourselves on tailoring our services to your needs at all stages of the complaints process. If we have not lived up to the very high standards we strive to attain, we apologise and would welcome the opportunity to discuss the problem further. If you're so angered by this platitudinous rot that you give up your complaint, that would be most welcome: as long as we maintain a high percentage of these apology 'wins' we can say in our annual report that our customers love us and the numbers prove it.'

THE SORRY ❛ SIDESTEP ❜

Instead of decisively stepping to one side or the other of an oncoming fellow pedestrian, we British tend to perform the elaborate SORRY 'SIDESTEP'. The moves are simple to follow and most natives will help you out if you go wrong. First, establish eye contact and wait for them to make their move to avoid you; mirror their move fractionally after them so that you are still on a collision course. Smile wryly and mouth 'SORRY' as you both move to the opposite side and continue on a bearing that will necessitate coming to a complete standstill. If you're both very practised, after this double sidestep you can push it a stage further so that you either end up bumping shoulders with very loud exclamations of 'SORRY', or else performing a last-minute shoulder turn to glide past your partner – a verbal apology and an embarrassed giggle are also appropriate at this stage.

❛ SORRY, IS ANYONE USING THIS? ❜

You find a table at a coffee shop but there are three of you and only two chairs. You look around and spot what might be a spare chair at an occupied table. Instead of a simple 'Hello, may I take that seat, please?' you say 'SORRY'. It's the equivalent of a throat clearance but, being British, we have to use our stalwart word instead.

You find yourself on holiday, in hostile territory, the sun beating down mercilessly – it must be at least 22 degrees out there. A stranger approaches and deploys his secret weapon – he speaks to you in his own language. You have barely enough time to register your affront before you realise he is asking you a question – you can tell this from his facial expression and the fact that he has stopped talking (thank God) and is now staring at you expectantly. For a moment you think he's got you; a trickle of sweat from your forehead mingles with Factor 50 sun cream and drips onto your upper lip. Aha! Adrenalin kicks in – Battle of Waterloo, Enigma Code, Concorde, Spice Girls – your proud heritage swells in your brain and forces out a retort: 'SORRY – I'M BRITISH.'

ACKNOWLEDGEMENTS

We'd like to thank, in no particular order, Nicola Barr, our terrific agent at Greene and Heaton, Malcolm Croft and the team at Anova, Kim, dad and Hannah for their help, contributions and for not glazing over every time we mentioned the book. Sammy and Maisie for their help with the 'Pets' chapter.

Finally, in the spirit of *Leaves on the Line*, we're really, really SORRY (see p.138) if we've missed anyone off this list.